Abandoned
by the Gods

4 fantasy shorts from the godless land of Adeva

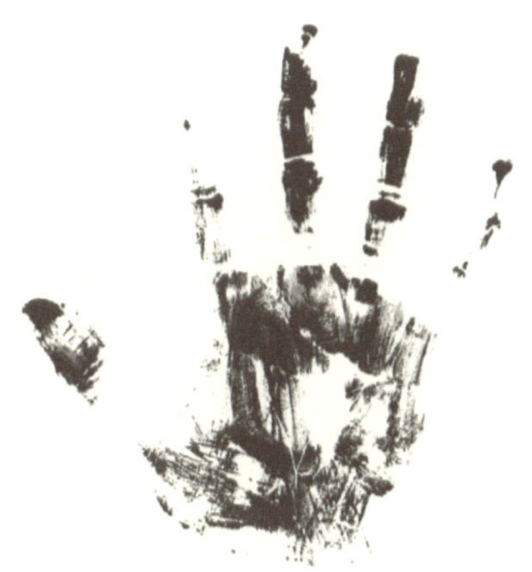

Ronit J

FOR THE READERS

I wouldn't be doing what I am doing if not for you

CONTENTS

Acknowledgments — i

Trigger Warnings — ii

Author's Note — iv

1 Servant of God — 1

2 The Princess Who Loved Her Maid — 45

3 Dacoit, Son of a Noble — 64

4 Bittersweet Chutney — 93

Thank you, readers! — 125

About the Author — 126

More by the Author — 127

ACKNOWLEDGMENTS

Once again, I want to begin by thanking my loving wife, Gopi. She has always been by my side, even when I first thought about working on these stories in 2022. Her eternal love and support have kept me going.

Secondly, I want to thank Alisha, Saurabh, and all my beta readers, whose generous feedback helped me make these stories better. Thank you for trusting me and giving my stories your time.

I also want to thank my parents for their undying love and support. If it weren't for all those books you bought me when I was a kid, I wouldn't be able to write all these books I have in my head.

And lastly, I want to thank my readers. I'm only just starting out, and I know the journey is long and hard. But it's also one that is deeply satisfying and you are an important reason why.

TRIGGER WARNINGS

Unlike my debut novel, the stories included in this collection are much darker and more serious in tone. Each of these stories contains elements that can be triggering. To give readers a chance to enjoy this book without discomfort, I'm including two Trigger Warnings, one that lists everything, and one that separates the warnings into individual stories.

OVERALL WARNINGS:

These stories contain strong language, blasphemy, hate speech, violence, gore, dismemberment, discrimination, casteism, classism, sexism, implied/off-page sexual assault, gaslighting, and domestic violence.

Individual warnings on the next page

INDIVIDUAL WARNINGS:

Servant of God:
strong language, blasphemy, violence, gore, discrimination, casteism, classism, sexism, implied/off-page sexual assault, and gaslighting.

The Princess Who Loved Her Maid:
strong language, blasphemy, discrimination, casteism, classism, sexism, and domestic violence.

Dacoit, Son of a Noble:
strong language, blasphemy, hate speech, violence, gore, and dismemberment.

Bittersweet Chutney:
strong language, blasphemy, hate speech, violence, gore, dismemberment, discrimination, and sexism.

AUTHOR'S NOTE

In 2022, I challenged myself to write one short story every month. By the end of August 2022, I had 12 rough drafts on my laptop. Of course, life got in the way, and I wasn't able to give these stories enough attention until early 2023 when I finally managed to find time and edit three of them.

In April 2023, the first of those stories—*Dacoit, Son of a Noble*—was selected for publication in *Dark Horses Magazine Nov 2023*. Coincidentally, April 2023 was also the month that I started working on what would become my debut novel—*Help! My Dog Is The Chosen One!*

The idea behind writing these 12 stories was to build the world of my main WIP. This is a world that I originally thought of in 2005 when I was eleven. Although this world has changed to the point of not resembling the original at all, some themes, ideas and concepts have remained with me. In 2021, I started reworking these ideas with book 1 of a new trilogy. This was the year Adeva was born. Sadly, I wasn't able to finish it because of a lot of different reasons.

By writing these short stories, I tackled two major writing hurdles—my gap in writing about Adeva, and my lack of time spent world-building. Writing these stories got me in the headspace to work on my main WIP again. Although I have about 100k words in book 1, I am in a position where I have to rewrite the whole thing because a lot has developed since the time I first wrote it.

However, with all the progress I have made as a writer and an author, I am confident I can pull this off. Not only will I finish writing these books, but I'll also be ready to share these stories with the world. Adeva is just one continent in this world, but it is the setting of my next trilogy. A godless land abandoned by the Gods over a thousand years ago.

The stories I wrote in 2022 were divided into two categories—1) episodes from the main characters' pasts, and 2) stories of individuals who lived their lives in the backdrop of Adeva's major events.

The stories collected here are from the latter category. I always found forgotten history and unsung heroes to be compelling themes. This anthology was my attempt at writing about some individuals whose lives were meaningful, some who even changed the course of history, but were forgotten for one reason or another.

Each story is a stand-alone, focusing on the characters and their world. The connections to the main series, while existent, aren't important to enjoy these stories. However, I do believe that if you revisit these stories later, you might find interesting easter eggs. I bet there are some connections between the stories themselves that you won't figure out in your first read. Only one of my beta readers did, and even they didn't catch everything.

If you wish to learn about the behind-the-scenes of writing these stories, I would recommend you check out my blog on www.ronitjauthor.com or my social media feed. I've written about my inspirations and process for writing each of these stories. In my blog post, I've also expanded on how and why I came about creating Adeva. It's not all positive, but it is all deeply personal.

That being said, I welcome you to my fantasy world of Adeva. It is inspired by mythological tales from India, but none of the culture is any real representation of Indian history or mythology. Everything written in this world is completely fabricated to tell the stories I want to tell, to explore the themes that matter to me, and to present a version of human life that I hope will compel you to reflect upon the world we live in.

I hope you enjoy reading these stories.

Ronit J
9 May 2024

SERVANT OF GOD

Jagadasi's parents were staunch devotees of Jagarakshaka the Protector, so much so that they *donated* her—their only daughter—to be a devadasi. A servant of god.

"But why?" she asked them, voice trembling with fear.

"Because," her mother replied softly, tying Jagadasi's sack, "It is the greatest of honours to serve the Protector!" The pride in her voice silenced Jagadasi. She couldn't even think of hurting them, not when they looked so eager.

But why her? Why couldn't it be any of the other kids?

"We don't choose, Jagadasi," her mother told her, "Jagarakshaka chooses. And you're fortunate to be chosen!" Had she read her mind? Or did she just say it to make her feel better?

"You're a big girl now," her father reassured her,

"You know? When I was ten, I would help my father plough the fields."

"I wish my parents had given me up for such a wonderful thing!" her mother added with a smile, "But now I see that my destiny was to birth you!"

"Come now," her father said with a teary smile, "It is time."

The neighbours held bronze plates with fruits and lamps, a final *aarti* to bid Jagadasi farewell. Her father had explained that her service to the gods would not only bring good fortune to her family but also to their whole community. Maybe that was why she was showered with fruits and grains for alms, too many for her little hands to carry.

Jagadasi couldn't help but smile back. What would they say if she cried? That she was ungrateful? That she was selfish? She couldn't bring such shame upon her family. This was her duty, and Jagarakshaka would reward her well for this.

Jagadasi stood there holding her fake smile, thanking every woman who offered her the protection of the flames, who showered her with grains of rice and applied turmeric and vermillion on her forehead. She smiled and thanked every man and every child who joined their hands in gratitude to her. Even the elders touched her feet despite her being so small.

When all was done, her parents knelt before her. They took a clay pot full of water and washed her feet with their own hands. After they were done, he father took the *pallu* of her sari. He looked at her with teary eyes, then tore it. That was the ritual.

He wrapped the small clay pot with the torn *pallu* of her sari and hung it from their cottage's door.

"Thank you, Jagadasi," her father said, "We will miss you."

Then, she was taken away to the Trinetra temple.

The Trinetra temple was one of Jagadasi's favourite places in their bustling village. It wasn't one of the eighteen pilgrimage sites for Jagarakshaka followers, but it was considered by many to be the unofficial nineteenth one. It even lent its name to their village, Trinetrapur.

The temple held the holy Trinetra idol—the three-eyed form of Jagarakshaka the Protector—that was such a marvel to look at. It brought hundreds of pilgrims from all over Adeva every year. It was a tiny idol carved from red sandstone, its eyes made of pearls, and its mien the most calming one she'd ever seen. Only a God could attain such absolute peace.

She was welcomed into the temple with a grand *puja* that no one attended except Pandit Jagadish, the head priest and Ura, the leader of the devadasis. She obeyed the priest and cleaned the idol with milk and water—her first act as a devadasi. With the cleansing, she had fully become, a servant of god.

After all was said and done, her father bid her farewell. Her mother hugged her one last time and then walked away without turning back. The last person they said their goodbyes to was Jagarakshaka. They wouldn't be allowed inside the temple compound again. As was the custom, a devadasi was expected to cut all ties with her life and her family. She would never see her parents again, lest she be tempted to renounce her holy service.

Jagadasi watched them go with a heavy heart and weeping eyes. They didn't even turn to look at her again.

She knew this was it. This was the moment that her old life ended.

"I have to... what?"

"What did you think a devadasi does?" Ura asked, listing out all of Jagadasi's chores for her.

Jagadasi had assumed that being a devadasi would mean taking care of Jagarakshaka. Chanting hymns, singing songs, and reciting stories of his divine feats. She thought life in the temple would be full of peace and helping patrons with holy duties.

Sadly, she was tasked with cleaning. Not just sweeping and mopping the temple floors, but also the compound, as well as their quarters. No matter how many times she raked away fallen leaves, there would always be more. She could sweep and mop till her bones ached, and the dust would return less than an hour later.

Jagadasi's little arms were too weak to handle the tasks, but she had no one to complain to. When she went up to Ura, all she got in return was a slap and a scolding. When she didn't sweep properly, she received a beating with her own broom. The worst was cleaning the kitchen quarters, where the stench of leftovers and rotting refuse was as bad as the latrines, not to mention the thick smoke that made her eyes water and throat itch.

Thankfully patrons weren't allowed to relieve themselves within the temple compounds; just the thought of having to clean strangers' waste made Jagadasi gag. The first year of her life as a devadasi was spent sweating and dirtying her hands so Jagarakshaka's temple could remain spick and span.

Jagadasi had slowly come to detest the other devadasis. There were only three others, but they didn't do anything other than gardening and singing. Often, rich merchants and patrons would come and pay for private sessions, where the devadasis would perform for hours. Singing songs of Jagarakshaka's glory while the temple musicians played holy music. Jagadasi wanted to be one of them. Ura didn't even perform any duty other than manage the devadasis. She did, however, perform for the richest of patrons.

One day, Jagadasi would take her place, she promised. Perform, sing, maybe dance, but nothing else.

Jagadasi didn't feel right about the activities the devadasis were engaged in *after* their performances. One night she overheard one patron referring to the temple as a *brothel*, and that made her want to beat him with her broom. How could anyone compare such a divine place with something so vile? Worse, how could the devadasis and temple attendants entertain people in that way? Why wasn't Jagarakshaka stopping any of them?

Fortunately, Jagadasi was spared those activities. But that only meant she had to work twice as hard with the clean-up. Since Jagadasi got so dirty every day from her duties, she wasn't allowed into the *mandapa* of the temple. Only once a week, she could enter and pray after she had bathed with oils and flowers. That year was very difficult for her, to be kept away from her beloved lord.

The second year, she was promoted to cleaning the *mandapa* and the *garbgruha*. She was allowed to get close to the Protector, and cleaning the temple floors didn't take up much time. So, once she was free, she was expected to help in the kitchens to prepare the delicious food that was given to patrons as offerings. Of course, she wasn't allowed to eat it, only Ura and the head cook were allowed to taste it.

Jagadasi's stomach rumbled every time she looked at the food, but all she received for her meals was boiled rice and plain daal. It broke her heart when she learned that the food she consumed was made in bulk, not just for the attendants and devadasis, but also as alms for beggars.

The only consolation for her was that she was very close to becoming one of the performers. One day, she too would dedicate all her time and effort to lead the devadasis and perform all the time in the name of Jagarakshaka.

By year three, Jagadasi had begun to grow into a woman. When she looked at boys, she felt a stirring inside her. She longed for love that many maidens from stories enjoyed. Would a prince come to take her away? Would she ever tend to a righteous warrior, who then would reveal himself to be an avatar of Jagarakshaka?

When she had her first moonblood, Ura explained to her what it meant to be a woman. Then, she explained why devadasis weren't allowed to be normal women, proceeding to give her a concoction that would leave her barren.

With trembling hands, she accepted the cup. "But... isn't this unnatural? What if Jagarakshaka wants me to be a moth—"

"We're not anyone's daughters or sisters or wives. We will never be mothers, or grandmothers, or great-grandmothers. We belong to no one."

Except Jagarakshaka.

"Now that you're a woman," Ura said, "You'll have to be careful around the men."

"What?"

Ura explained what she meant, and Jagadasi couldn't help but feel repulsed. "Why do we let such people in then?"

"People? Even the priests can be bloody perverts!" Ura said with venom in her voice. "The only reason no one touched you yet was because you were a child. But you aren't anymore."

Jagadasi heard the warning. Pale, forlorn, Jagadasi drank her cup, all the while praying to Jagarakshaka, *Please! Protect me my beloved!*

It didn't take long for Pandit Jagadish to request her presence in his chamber at night. He didn't let her leave until sunrise.

Eight months into her new duties, Jagadasi still wasn't able to cope. She sat before the Trinetra idol, trying hard to let its calm seep into her. She had been trying for over an hour, but failed.

Her insides trembled with fear and shame. She whispered quietly, "Why me? I'm sorry for asking this of you, but why me?"

Jagarakshaka didn't respond. He kept looking at her with his pearly three-eyed gaze.

"What did I do wrong to end up here? Am I being punished for some sin from my past life? I always thought that devadasis were honourable people, but this feels like a punishment—"

"How old were you when they sold you?"

Jagadasi went pale.

Had someone been eavesdropping? Had she just blasphemed before...

Without turning, she stood up slowly. Her gaze remained on Jagarakshaka, full of regret and shame.

"Girl?" a hand gently grabbed her shoulder and turned her around. "I asked you a question."

"I was only practising for a play," Jagadasi blurted. "I'm sorry, I just find it easy to do it before the idol. Ura always reprim—"

The fat man before her gently put his finger on her lips. "Don't lie in Jagarakshaka's house, my dear." He leaned forward and whispered, "You aren't mistaken when you think this is a punishment."

Jagadasi went pale. To blaspheme was a sin, but repenting could cleanse her. She couldn't allow this fat man to corrupt her soul further.

"Did you know that the devadasi pratha had

started as a means to keep the temples functioning? Has anyone told you of the history of the devadasis?"

Jagadasi shook her head. The only education she had received was devotion and service of Jagarakshaka.

"Come with me," the fat man offered her a hand, "No one will say anything to you. I'm a priest myself."

Jagadasi noticed his robes, but he didn't wear any adornments. Where were his *rudrakshmalas*? His vermillion or sandalwood *tilaks*? Suspicious, Jagadasi said, "I'm sorry, but…"

"Don't be," the fat man smiled, "Any layman can smear colours on their forehead to look like a priest. It takes a truly learned man to become one."

"But…"

"Besides, I know all about the dirty things this temple is engaged in. It's sad if you ask me. But then again, the temple's patronage has been poor since King Vjaijnan started his Uniting Crusade."

His words flew over her head like the seasonal birds whose names she had never learned.

"Do you agree with all the services the priests ask of you?"

That she understood. The heat in her cheeks betrayed her thoughts.

"So, I was right," the fat man—priest—shook his head regretfully. "The times are changing. And you are one of the many unfortunates whose lives will be uprooted in the maelstrom that is sure to come, Jagadasi."

Did I tell him my name? Did one of the other priests? Jagadasi shook her head and claimed, "Jagarakshaka will protect me."

"Are you sure?"

Jagarakshaka will protect me! But he failed to protect her from Pandit Jagadish.

He protects everyone. He hadn't stopped anyone from making her a devadasi.

Please help me. I need help. I know you are listening.

"I AM LISTENING!"

Jagadasi's heart skipped a beat, a void enlarging within her as goosebumps mottled her flesh.

"I AM LISTENING TO ALL OF YOU!"

Her mouth went dry. She could hear him. But his voice...

"Let's go see what is happening over there," the fat priest said, walking away without looking back.

Jagadasi, curious about the voice, followed him towards the entrance of the temple. A small crowd had entered the courtyard and were making their way up the steps to enter the *mandapa*. They didn't touch the threshold, or ring any bells; they were preoccupied with holding a woman that screamed maniacally. "THE GODS ARE LISTENING. I AM THEIR OBSERVER!"

Jagadasi had seen this happen many times in her life, but only during *pujas*. They said that matron goddesses of the earth would enter pure women during holy rituals to grant blessings.

But, there wasn't any *puja* being conducted. It was just a regular day.

"Mataji is here!" one of the men holding the woman called out.

"Shut up you fool!" snapped another, an older balding man who seemed to be struggling to keep his hold. "Goddesses don't possess women randomly. This is a wicked spirit!"

"I CAN HEAR YOU! I CAN SEE YOU! I SEE ALL!"

A junior priest looked dumbfounded, "Let me get Pandit Jagadish."

"No need," the fat priest said, raising a hand. "I

am a Pandit myself. I can take care of this."

"LIAR! LIAR!" the woman screamed, pointing an accusatory finger at him.

The fat priest sighed and slapped her hard across the face. "No god would accuse a priest like that. This is surely a wicked spirit."

"LI—"

SLAP.

The woman held her cheek, frozen in shock. The fat priest chanted some hymns in the old tongue and raised his hand again.

The woman flinched.

"BEGONE!" the fat priest screamed in fury as he slapped her a third and final time. The slap was loud, echoing across the temple courtyard.

Jagadasi watched as the woman—*is that Auntie Dhara?*—fall unconscious. The man holding her—*Uncle Binod!*—held her up as her body slumped into his arms.

"What did you do!?" the old man—*Grandpa Shloka!*—shouted at the fat priest.

"Slapped the wicked spirit out of her blessed body," the fat priest responded with joined hands. "You are quite welcome. You can thank Jagarakshaka for protecting us all."

"You just slapped my daughter-in-law! She..."

"Is there a problem?" Pandit Jagadish walked up to the crowd along with Ura and some junior priests. He had just returned from a bath in the river.

"Just a simple case of spirit possession," the fat priest replied, "Nothing to worry about."

"He slapped my daughter-in-law!" Grandpa Shloka accused.

The head priest studied the fat man for a second, before recognising, "Pandit Punyamaan?"

"You must be Pandit Jagadish," the fat priest—Punyamaan—joined his hands. "I wrote to you a few months ago."

The crowd's demeanour changed almost instantaneously. Grandpa Shloka's animosity, Uncle Binod's worry, and Jagadasi's confusion, all melted away as the realisation of Pandit Punyamaan's identity settled in. From scepticism to awe, the crowd began showering their praises and thanks to the Pandit.

Jagadasi couldn't believe herself. Had she really doubted this godly man? She felt an intense need to make up for her impudence.

Suddenly, Auntie Dhara began convulsing. Slowly, she opened her eyes, looking around her like she was in a trance. "Where am I?"

"Daughter," the head priest said, "You are in the home of Jagarakshaka the Protector. Can you see his Trinetra form there?" He pointed to the *garbgruha*.

She looked and nodded, tears in her eyes.

"You were possessed by a stray spirit. But fear not, Jagarakshaka has protected you. Now pay your respects and thank him for his protection."

"Don't forget about me," Pandit Punyamaan teased, "Or else I'll slap you again," he raised his hand in mockery.

The crowd laughed. An oddly animated response for what wasn't even a very funny jest.

Auntie Dhara obeyed. Flanked by Uncle Binod and Grandpa Shloka, she rang the temple bells, walked over to the Trinetra idol and prostrated before it. While they engaged in prayers, Jagadasi waited patiently. She wasn't allowed to meet her parents, but the rules didn't say anything about distant cousins. All these years, she had never had any relative visit the temple. She had met neighbours, had met people she recognised, but for once an actual family member had come to visit!

Jagadasi watched as Uncle Binod emptied his

pockets into the temple's donation box. The younger Jagadasi would've thought him generous, but living in the temple had taught her better. Junior priests hovered around him, greedily urging him to pour all his money in.

After Uncle Binod showed them his empty pockets, they finally 'blessed' him and left. Uncle Binod joined his hands in prayer one last time and began descending the temple steps.

Jagadasi made sure that the two Pandits and Ura were busy talking. No one else was watching, so she slowly followed her relatives. As he joined his wife and father, Jagadasi called out, "Uncle Binod! Auntie Dhara!"

They stiffened, turning to see who was calling. She couldn't remember the last time she had seen them.

"It's me, Jagadasi!"

"Oh, Dasi." There was no excitement in her auntie's voice. "I forgot your parents sold you to the temple."

Sold? She faked a smile. "I volunteered, actually."

"Of course!" her Auntie said with a wave of her hand, "I misspoke."

Or maybe you didn't. "How are they?"

"I don't know. After they sol—" she cleared her throat, "after you were brought here, they left Trinetrapur. We don't know where they went. I'm sorry." She looked spent, sweat patching her blouse, hair in disarray. She wiped her nose and said, "I'm sorry, I have to go." And just like that, she left. She didn't even bid her farewell.

"Devadasis used to be a respected lot."

Jagadasi turned to find Pandit Punyamaan behind her. She hadn't heard him approaching. "What happened then?"

"As with all things pure and beautiful... people

found ways to exploit it."

"You mean the rich traders, kings…"

"Priests," he nodded sadly. "Not all of us are as pure as people believe."

Jagadasi wanted to leave, but didn't know how to excuse herself. "I think I have…"

"Your auntie was pretending, you know?"

Jagadasi hesitated. "What?"

"Many of these 'devotees' like to pretend that they are possessed."

"But…"

"I haven't seen a single possession where I could sense a divine or otherworldly presence. It's all a… how can I say this without sounding blasphemous… a broken mind's way of screaming for attention. Like a crying baby, but worse."

"But…"

"Jagadasi," he said fondly, "I can sense that you are purer than anyone else. You truly love Jagarakshaka, don't you?"

Nervously, she nodded.

"Then you have to help me cleanse this place."

"W-what?"

"You know exactly what I'm talking about."

"Pandit Punyamaan! Is she troubling you?" Pandit Jagadish asked from afar.

"Troubling? Not at all! I was just complimenting her for her purity."

"Purity?" the head priest shot her a glance.

"I can sense Jagarakshaka's blessing on her. She is a special one."

Pandit Jagadish nodded, unconvinced. "Maybe because she started so young. You know how the times have changed. War is in the air."

"So are disease, famine, and many other issues."

"How long will you be staying with us?"

"As long as Jagarakshaka wants me to!" he said,

raising his hands to the air, then joining them in prayer.

Pandit Jagadish didn't look pleased with that.

That night, Jagadasi was abruptly woken up. "Pandit Jagadish is no more…"

"W-what?"

Ura clicked her tongue, "He passed in his sleep. Get up now!"

While the junior priests and devadasis mourned the head priest, Jagadasi was tasked with fetching water for the arrivals. Although serving the others wasn't new to her, something felt off. The air was quiet, as it should be after death. But there was also something unspoken, something eerie. Jagadasi couldn't help but feel suspicious, and she didn't know why.

The most experienced of the junior priests had taken charge, giving instructions on what needed to be done. Jagadasi had never seen a funeral in her life. She had heard of funerals, had known about death, but never had she witnessed one.

She felt nothing.

After what the head priest had done, he didn't deserve half the respect he was getting. Was that why she was feeling unsettled? *No… something* is *wrong.*

"What are you glaring at?" Ura hissed and walked over to her. "The Sarpanch will be here, as well as some prominent names from Trinetrapur. You better not act like that, you hear me?"

Despite herself, Jagadasi clenched her jaw and nodded. Her anger slowly poured tears out of her eyes. Convenient, because the devadasis were expected to cry. No other women were allowed to touch the body.

Jagadasi wanted to spit on Pandit Jagadish's face, but managed to hold herself together. As respectfully as she could, she helped Ura anoint the body with oil, rosewater, and herbs. By the time the junior priests had said their final prayers, Pandit Punyamaan arrived with the Sarpanch, the village headman.

As the Sarpanch paid his respects, Jagadasi looked at Pandit Punyamaan. He had assumed charge and was instruction the junior priests. It made sense, given his title of Pandit, but did that also mean he was going to replace the head priest?

A few more prominent villagers came to pay their respects, after which the men left with the deceased, while the devadasis were left behind. They didn't talk to each other, but Ura ordered them all to bathe and cleanse themselves of death's aura. Jagadasi obeyed and was the last to leave the river. No one bothered her because they assumed she missed the head priest.

Do they actually think I had feelings for that pervert?

When she returned, she found the men back. The Sarpanch requested Pandit Punyamaan to take charge of the temple while they looked for another head priest. He was quick to take the offer, which to Jagadasi felt odd. This man had come out of nowhere, and now he was being offered the position of head priest?

The old head priest had died the same day this man had arrived. Did no one else suspect something wrong? Why was Jagadasi being so suspicious and sceptical? Her mind had been unsettled all throughout the funeral.

After the villagers left, Pandit Punyamaan dismissed everyone, except Jagadasi. No one questioned him, but Jagadasi wasn't going to silently obey. She followed him to his room, and when he closed the door behind him, she just stood there with her fists balled.

"I'm not asking you to sleep with me," the fat priest said.

That didn't ease her mind one bit. But she didn't know what to say, so she let him continue.

"I know what you're thinking. And you're right. I killed him."

Hearing her doubts confirmed sent a chill down her spine. "What?"

"I killed the bastard."

Jagadasi had never heard a priest curse like that.

"I told you, you have to help me cleanse this place. If you do, Jagarakshaka will be very happy."

Her mind suddenly went silent. She was breathing slowly, her heart beating fast. She wanted to cleanse the temple of all its ill-doings, of all the blasphemous things that the priests and devadasis engaged in despite their ungodly nature. *Jagarakshaka would want me to cleanse the temple.* "But... how?"

Pandit Punyamaan smiled kindly, "I'll explain."

Pandit Punyamaan's plan to clean up the temple should have frightened Jagadasi. But, having had her share of blasphemous thoughts, she saw it as a necessity. What did she know? She was just a child.

The very next morning, Jagadasi volunteered for gardening duties. As instructed. Although she was only given small blades and spades to work with, they were sharp enough. She decided she would spend some time practising how the tools worked in her hands.

Pandit Punyamaan had only told her how to use the tools, but his words had worked like magic. As if

Jagarakshaka himself had blessed Jagadasi with the manoeuvrability needed to master the use of these tools.

Along with acclimatising herself to the tools, Jagadasi made sure to practise all the hymns and stories of Jagarakshaka. After all, this was meant to be a cleansing. For the purity of the world. For the purity of the temple. For Jagarakshaka.

Months passed by. While Jagadasi was tasked with practice, Pandit Punyamaan's temporary substitution meant the temple's secret activities had to be paused. And their effects were made clear by the depleting funds.

Ura and the junior priests didn't trust Punyamaan enough to openly suggest their solutions, which made them increasingly frustrated. The only way to resolve this was be to bring in priests from outside to replace Pandit Jagadish, but Pandit Punyamaan's high standards found all their candidates grossly wanting.

Jagadasi felt glee upon seeing the nasty temple workers failing at resuming their corrupt activities. Soon the temple would be clean. Soon it would be reinstated to its former glory.

I trust you, Jagadasi. I can sense the purity inside you. Jagarakshaka has chosen you!

The day of cleansing was nearing, and she couldn't wait.

The day finally arrived. Pandit Punyamaan had made sure that everyone in the temple had been working hard. Them being exhausted would make Jagadasi's work easier. The sun was about to set, and the temple had been closed early so Punyamaan could perform a cleansing *puja* for Pandit Jagadish's soul to finally rest.

Everyone was inside the temple. Those who

weren't busy had gathered outside the *garbgruha* to witness the *puja*.

As instructed, Jagadasi ignored everyone, went straight into the *garbgruha* and sat next to Punyamaan. The ritual fire blazed before the Trinetra idol, and Jagadasi could see the desire for cleansing within Jagarakshaka's pearly eyes.

Seemingly out of nowhere, Pandit Punyamaan placed a sickle onto Jagadasi's lap and whispered, "Whenever you are ready, my sweet Jagadasi."

Jagadasi felt her heart skip a beat. She looked at the sickle, then at the Trinetra idol. *Protect me, Jagarakshaka. I'm doing this for you.*

"It is time."

As if those words were Jagarakshaka's command, Jagadasi's entire body sparked alive with fire. All her nervousness, all her qualms, all her innate need to be polite and caring melted away. In their place came anger, disgust, all her animosity against this temple's blasphemy. It screamed in her head. It was unnatural, as if someone outside her body was pulling at strings in her mind. It didn't matter. She felt powerful. Intoxicated by that sheer brutal power, Jagadasi gripped the sickle tightly and started up.

She let out a cackle. "Hahahahahahahaha." She flared her hands about, letting the sickle into sight. "Hehehehehehe." She gripped the sickle firmer and turned, eyes bulging red, tongue lolling out. "Rararararararararararara—" one step forward "—rararararararara—" second step, third step. The sickle rose above her head, casting an ominous shadow on the onlookers.

The audience went pale. Silence filled the air, except Pandit Punyamaan's low chants. He was unbothered by Jagadasi's sudden transformation.

"Pandit!" Ura screamed, "Jagadasi...."

"LALALALALALALA!" Jagadasi howled and

swung the sickle. The arc was perfect, the blade freshly sharpened. It hissed through the air, threatening like a snake.

"Jagadasi, what are you doing!?" Ura screamed, but her scolding had no effect on Jagadasi.

Jagadasi stepped closer and swung the sickle a few times threateningly.

When Ura realised what was happening, she let her guard down. "Jagadasi..."

Jagadasi lopped her head off. It thudded to the floor, followed by a soft plop of Ura's body. Jagadasi smiled, feeling triumphant. Loudly, she bellowed, "JAGARAKSAHKA PUNISHES YOU!"

Screams erupted from the crowd. Junior priests, attendants, and the devadasis all scrambled away as the mad woman ran towards them.

"I am doing God's work!" she slashed at the escaping priests. Pleasure exploded in her stomach at the feeling of her sickle digging into their flesh. She found herself slipping into a daze.

"Jagarakshaka punishes you!" she took a step forward, "You vile insects have defiled the holy house of Trinetra Jagarakshaka! You must pay!"

The attendants jumped her, pulled at her pallu, but she simply sliced it off and stabbed one of the attendants. "YOU DARE!?"

The others jumped on her and they all crashed to the floor. Jagadasi screamed her throat raw. Without thinking, she grabbed the face of the junior priest on top of her and pushed her thumbs into his eyes. Warm gooey liquid oozed out as he screamed for help. She snatched the sickle from the ground and hacked at him.

As she rose to her feet, she saw that her acts had scared everyone away. Auntie Dhara had just been loud and abusive. Jagadasi was horror come alive. She had spent so many hours scrubbing the stone floors clean, her muscles must have hardened with the labour. Now she would use those built muscles to paint the same floors red with the blood of these heathens.

Jagarakshaka has blessed me! Godly energy coursed through her veins, pumped her muscles with divine strength.

"JAGARAKSHAKA HAS COME TO ME! HE IS DISGUSTED WITH YOU, AND HAS ASKED ME TO PUNISH YOU! COME, ACCEPT HIS PUNISHMENT!"

Behind her, Pandit Punyamaan continued to perform the *puja*, peacefully chanting praises to the Protector.

An hour later, Jagadasi trudged towards the *garbgruha*, walked past Pandit Punyamaan, and prostrated before Trinetra's idol. Her clothes were in tatters, the blood of the blasphemers splattered all over her. The bloodied sickle lay next to her, reflecting the slaughter that had drenched her soul.

The sun had fully set, leaving the world in darkness on that moonless night. The only light in the temple was from the fires that Jagadasi had set to the bodies of the blasphemers.

"Thank you for protecting me, Jagarakshaka."

The three-eyed Protector with his red sandalwood mien and pearly eyes looked at her. She could almost sense his presence in the temple.

"I will cleanse this world. You will help me, yes?"

"Pandit Punyamaan?" a soft murmur called.

She grabbed the sickle and started up. But the energy within her wasn't nearly as potent as before. She was tired. Her muscles ached, crying for respite. Before her, she saw a crowd of villagers gathered. The voice that called out was the Sarpanch.

Pandit Punyamaan stepped between them. "Easy,

child. You have done well."

"Panditji?" the village headman repeated, "What happened here?"

"What I had hoped to avoid all this time," Pandit Punyamaan's voice was heavy with sorrow. Jagadasi's own eyes leaked tears she didn't know she had inside her.

The Sarpanch looked to his own feet, "I am ashamed, Panditji. I was against it from the start, but Pandit Jagdish..."

"No need to explain yourself, Sarpanchji," Punyamaan waved his chubby hands before him, "The *puja* I conducted today has accomplished its purpose. And, it appears that Jagarakshaka has blessed us all..." he gestured to Jagadasi.

"Blessed?" The Sarpanch's tone was sceptical.

Jagadasi wiped the blood off her cheek, but only ended up smearing more across her face. It was starting to smell, and she wanted to bathe. But it appeared she still had a role to play.

"Why, yes! You see, the moment I was close to concluding the main portion of the *puja*, Jagadasi here was possessed by a spirit."

"Possessed?"

"Indeed! It seems she was *blessed* by a particularly strong goddess because she was able to cull all the filth in less than an hour."

"But..."

"Jagadasi's only fourteen, Sarpanchji. You don't really think a fourteen-year-old could slaughter *all* the staff by herself, do you?"

"N-no..."

Pandit Punyamaan turned to her and bowed with joined hands, "I am eternally grateful for your arrival, Mataji."

Did he call me Mataji? Unsure what to do, she joined her hands and bowed.

The Sarpanch followed suit. Behind him, the villagers stood with pale faces and unblinking eyes. They bowed in fear as well, not questioning the Pandit's words.

Suddenly, the horror of her actions slapped Jagadasi across her face. The fluttering in her stomach turned to shame, the pleasure turned to disgust.

No! I did it for Jagarakshaka!

"Address them, Mataji," Pandit Punyamaan said. His warm voice silenced the storm in her mind. She knew this moment would come. She had practised for it.

"This temple..." she said, voice quivering, "... had become..." *You did nothing wrong,* "... a place of blasphemy."

The Sarpanch nodded slowly, waiting for her to continue. They all waited. They had never let her speak before. Pandit Punyamaan nodded his approval.

She gulped and continued, "Jagarakshaka," her voice found ground to stand firmly on, "gave me a choice. To kill the blasphemers, or... continue to do the bad things they made me do." Jagadasi grimaced, feeling anger bubble inside her. "Your so-called *high priest* was a vile man. He forced me to sleep with him every night! The only reason he didn't sell me to patrons was because he wanted me all to himself!" She suddenly spread her arms out, causing the crowd to gasp, "The attendants, the junior priests, the devadasis, were nothing more than corrupt men and women." She pointed an accusing finger at them, "They stole your money! They insulted the name of Jagarakshaka! Jagarakshaka is upset. He called to me because I was pure."

A memory nudged her, and she searched the crowd. Everyone unconsciously took a step back as she walked through them, the blood-caked sickle stinking of death.

Jagadasi found who she was looking for, "Auntie Dhara!" she pointed with her sickle, "You were possessed a few months ago." She shook her head, "They made you pay, didn't they? They claimed to have cured you, but it was Pandit Punyamaan who drove the spirit away!"

Auntie Dhara, frightened and weeping. "Yes, Mataji!"

"They claimed to do the work of God, but they were nothing more than greedy pigs! THAT..." she spun around, pointing her sickle at Jagarakshaka, "is why he chose me. To undo their doing. To kill the wicked ones." She looked at everyone, making sure to meet their eyes. The way they averted their gaze made her smile. It pleased her to torment them with mere words. "Are you one of those vile men? Are you here to kill me? Grab me and fuck me so the world can return to its blaspheming?" That was the first time she had cussed, and it felt good. The word had power, and it reminded her how strong and divine she had felt when slaughtering the temple workers.

"TELL ME!"

The crowd flinched.

"TELL ME!" she repeated, this time slicing the air with her bloodstained sickle for effect. It amused her to see how easy it was to control these people.

The Sarpanch braved forward. "Mataji, some attendants from the temple rushed into my house, warning of a demon."

"Demon?" she let the word crack an ominous smile on her face. The Sarpanch almost jumped. She had to stifle her laughter.

"But we didn't believe them! A little girl killing so many? That sounded impossible. But..."

She looked at Pandit Punyamaan. He just blinked

once.

"Where are they?" she asked, accepting the authority she had just been granted.

"They..."

"Bring me their heads." It didn't even surprise her how easily she demanded it.

The villagers exchanged anxious glances.

Jagadasi raised the bloodied sickle, "FOR JAGARAKSHAKA!"

When the villagers returned with the heads of the escaped attendants, they found Jagadasi singing to Jagarakshaka. Some villagers dared to sit with her, while others went away, terrified out of their wits.

It had been a strange night.

To Jagadasi's favour, the villagers that did stay witnessed her sing one thousand verses of the *Jagarakshaka Puran*. The full text consisted of twenty-three thousand verses, of which Jagadasi knew only three thousand. But it was enough to impress the villagers, enough to convince them that she was truly blessed by the Protector himself.

When the three-thousandth verse left her tongue, she paused. Then meekly declared, "Aum Jai Jagarakshaka!" *Victory to Jagarakshaka!*

Pandit Punyamaan fiercely repeated, "Aum Jai Jagarakshaka!"

The villagers chanted after them. Hesitantly at first, then with more vigour believing they had witnessed a true miracle.

As the sun rose, Jagadasi found herself surrounded by worshippers. Some women from the village bathed her, got her a new sari to wear. They made fresh breakfast and turmeric milk for her, while the men cleaned the temple of the filth from the night before.

Never before in her life had she felt so much glee.

The tasks that she would perform like a slave, that threatened to break her tiny back, that calloused her hands and caused her pain, were now being done *for* her. She was no longer a servant. Instead, the world was now serving her.

She didn't even feel pity for the men who sweated to scrub the blood clean, who had to pick up the remains of the burnt bodies, or even the women who had to cook and serve her.

After finishing her breakfast, she met with Pandit Punyamaan, who praised her for her actions. "I cannot believe my eyes, Jagadasi! A real miracle! Jagarakshaka has truly blessed you!"

Jagadasi touched his feet and sought his blessing.

"No!" he stopped her, pulling her up straight, "You bow to no one, Jagadasi."

"But..."

"*This*," he gently joined his hands and bowed to her, "is your reward for being a devout follower. Despite everything, you stuck to the ways of *dharma* and upheld the pure teachings of Jagarakshaka. You have earned this, Jagadasi."

Jagadasi gulped, feeling her veins charged with the power she had displayed the night before. "What now, Panditji?"

"Now, we re-establish the grandeur of the Trinetra Temple. With *you* as the head priestess."

"But..."

"You have been blessed, Jagadasi. And you know all the scriptures. The ones you don't... you can always learn. But it doesn't matter. People will come hearing tales of your deeds. Of how you cleansed a corrupt temple in the name of the Protector." He took a step closer and held her tightly by the arms, "You will become an influential figure whose name shall echo in all of Adeva. And with your influence, you shall uphold the greatness of Jagarakshaka!"

Jagadasi longed for that. She had never dreamed of it before, but hearing Pandit Punyamaan speak, she desired it. She wanted power and influence, but most importantly, "Will they respect me? Treat me as—"

"Yes! I promise you. I will be by your side, making sure you have all the counsel you need. For as long as you need it."

Jagadasi didn't have to consider. She didn't know she had the right to. She just nodded and agreed without thinking, "Tell me what to do next."

"What do *you* want to do, Jagadasi? Today is *your* day."

She thought carefully. "I'm no longer a devadasi, right?"

"No. From today, you shall be a Pandita."

"But... I don't belong to the priest caste."

Punyamaan smiled, "When the Gods themselves meddle in our matters, exceptions can be made."

She nodded, understanding what he was saying. It was a warm feeling. After some thought, she asked, "Can I visit my parents?"

Pandit Punyamaan frowned, "Of course, Jagadasi. Are they in the village?"

"No. Auntie Dhara told me they left." She thought about it, "Maybe the Sarpanch knows something."

"Then you should summon him."

Me! Summon the village headman? Jagadasi's heart fluttered. "Yes, tell him I have requested his presence."

Pandit Punyamaan smiled and winked, "You mean *demanded*?"

Jagadasi looked at her old cottage. Memories of her happy childhood, of her life before she was sold to the temple, danced in her mind. She looked at the tree she would climb every evening to look at the sunset, the little cattle shed where they kept their weak livestock, the veranda where she played with her toys, where she was made to sit as the villagers and her family worshipped her, then sold her to the temple.

The pot tied with her torn *pallu* from her last day in the cottage still hung over the door. It had faded and was coated in a thick layer of dust. Had they not bothered to clean it? Wasn't it supposed to be holy?

"The last I heard, they were..." The Sarpanch hesitated, careful not to offend her, "They weren't particularly good people, Mataji."

"What do you mean?"

"I don't think it would be wise to—"

"She asked you a question," Pandit Punyamaan pushed.

Hesitantly, the Sarpanch continued, "They always fought. He beat her. She cursed him. They..." he avoided Jagadasi's gaze, "T-t-they apparently sold her to the temple because they couldn't afford to take care of her."

"That explains why she started so young," Pandit Punyamaan nodded.

"They wanted a boy, but they weren't able to conceive after her. And they..." The Sarpanch looked to his feet, "After they sold her, they used the money to leave the village. Last I heard, the mother was sentenced to death for killing the father."

"Why?" Jagadasi demanded, not reining in her anger.

Shamefacedly, the Sarpanch replied, "He tried to sell her into prostitution. It was a shame, those two. Forced into marriage by his mother, and now..." he shook his head and cleared his throat. "They never sold the house, so it's Trinetrapur's property. Since you're no longer a devadasi, you could—"

"Burn it."

"Mataji?"

"I think it's clear what she said, Sarpanchji," Pandit Punyamaan replied, "It seems that after everything, she wants to cleanse her past as well.

The Sarpanch nodded. A while later, two of the youngsters from the village walked about, setting fire to the abandoned house.

Like the bodies in the temple, like the lamps that were lit in Jagarakshaka's honour, her childhood home erupted in flames. She stood there watching. Her childhood had been snatched away by the very parents that she loved and respected. She trusted them to know best, and they had sold her like cattle in the market. Sold her to be a slave under the guise of devotion.

No. I am no longer a slave. I am no longer a weakling. I will take what I am owed. Starting today.

Stories of a fourteen-year-old girl massacring all the corrupt temple workers spread throughout Adeva like wildfire. Jagadasi received praise, worship, and support from devout folk from across classes. New priests and attendants came to the temple, some by invitation, others voluntarily. There was no shortage of volunteers to work for a temple blessed by Jagarakshaka himself.

Within a month, more people started coming to Trinetrapur. Pilgrims found one more reason to visit the sacred temple. People flooded Jagadasi for blessings, for good luck and whatever little message they would have for Jagarakshaka. All she had to do was say some reassuring words and bless them, and she would receive offerings in exchange. By the end of her first month as a Pandita, she had become the richest person in Trinetrapur.

And every time she thought someone was coming

close to cheating her, stealing her money, or trying to manipulate her, all she had to do was declare the cheat and her devotees would punish the perpetrator without question.

While Jagadasi blessed and engaged with the visitors, Pandit Punyamaan performed all the priestly duties. With his wisdom and knowledge, he guided her in making the right decisions. He was the father she never had. She was grateful to Jagarakshaka that their paths had crossed.

By the end of the year, Pandita Jagadasi had gained so many devotees that even rich merchants and smaller noble houses began sending her patronage. Soon they requested her presence, requested she sing and perform for them. Perform *only* in devotion to Jagarakshaka.

It felt right.

At the end of every performance, she was showered with gold and riches. Of course, she couldn't accept them herself; her attendants took care of that. After the performances, the nobles would confer with her and Pandit Punyamaan, seeking advice on political matters. It was in those meetings that Jagadasi truly understood what power meant.

They didn't just want her advice, they begged for it. They begged for her blessings so they could succeed in their endeavours, and she would give it to them, for a price. If the ask sounded moral to her, she would bless them. If not, she would refuse. Of course, Pandit Punyamaan helped her make those decisions, and she listened to him intently.

For once, her life was starting to seem comfortable.

Years passed, and Pandita Jagadasi became one of the most prominent spiritual leaders of Adeva. Her devotees numbered in the thousands. Even kings and queens and their royal brood had begun requesting her presence.

She was asked to bless their armies, to grant them luck, to grant them Jagarakshaka's favour. When Jagadasi gave audience to such, she received impossible riches in return. Despite being a simple priestess, she had a hermitage built for her right next to the Trinetra Temple. That *humble abode* was designed by a royal architect. Funded by riches from kings and nobles, it could put some royal palaces to shame.

In that hermitage, Jagadasi invited devadasis from around Adeva, freeing them of their bondage. Although she had grown greedy, she had found a calling other than her worship for Jagarakshaka. Her attempts to abolish the devadasi system invited scorn, insults and denouncements from many schools of thought. High priests, nobles, and even some kings found it blasphemous, but she knew what she was doing.

Along with Jagadasi's influence, the temple complex too expanded. Trinetrapur had generously donated land so the temple could build lodgings for travelling priests and devotees, install bigger kitchens, add a hall for community meals, and much more. While the main temple complex remained unchanged, the newer amenities were added in an extended perimeter, made by the best temple architects of Adeva and made to resemble the ancient architectural style of the temple. To the layman, the extended portions would look like they had been part of the temple for centuries.

On the four-year anniversary of her cleansing, Jagadasi was informed by Pandit Punyamaan that she had grown rich and influential enough that a king who was about to embark on his Uniting Crusade had requested her presence.

"What is the Uniting Crusade?" she asked him. She had heard the term a few times, but never bothered to ask.

"Jagadasi, you know how the Gods left Adeva?"

"Yes."

"Well, they left with a boon on this land. Anyone who can unite all of Adeva will be granted godhood."

"And anyone can embark on this crusade?"

"Not just anyone," Pandit Punyamaan clarified, "They have to perform certain rites. And with the conquest of each kingdom and each region, they have to perform *pujas* to consecrate their rule. This king has just begun his crusade, and wishes for your blessings."

"Is he a good king?"

"He is!" Pandit Punyamaan said, "After all, he has already won three kingdoms with just diplomacy."

"Is that so?"

"Yes. Only a noble king could achieve that, don't you think?"

Jagadasi played with her embroidered sari, thinking if Jagarakshaka approved of this king. "What if *we* embarked on the crusade?"

"Jagadasi?"

"If we can unite Adeva in the name of Jagarakshaka, can you imagine...?"

"You cannot lead a crusade, Jagadasi. You are not a queen. Besides, only kings have led crusades in the past. You know the story of Emperor Mahamara."

"An avatar of Jagarakshaka himself. I know. But,

why can't I lead? I am blessed by Jagarakshaka too! You said it yourself."

For the first time in years, Jagadasi saw Pandit Punyamaan frown. "This is not the way of *dharma*, Jagadasi. Your duty is to bless and inspire people. The kings of Adeva have their sacred duty to lead its people. Don't try to mix the two—"

"I was born a lowly villager. I was sold to be a slave. I've changed my caste and acted as Jagarakshaka demanded. Why can't I do this?"

"Jagadasi!" Punyamaan's voice was stern. "Women aren't allowed to embark on crusades."

"Is that what's written in the scriptures?" Jagadasi demanded.

The frown grew gaunt. "You dare question *me* about the scriptures?"

"Show me where in the scriptures it says that a woman can't lead the Uniting Crusade. I demand proof!"

A shadow fell on Punyamaan's face, darkening his eyes. The whole room seemed to dim as he took a threatening step forward. "The scriptures are written for our benefit, Jagadasi. And Pandits like me have studied those scriptures longer than you have been alive. Are you insinuating that your uneducated mind with its limited faculties is equipped to interpret, question and dismiss the scriptures written by enlightened intellectuals of ancient times?"

Every single word was like a needle pricking into her soul. Every single one of his words hurt her, shamed her, made her want to prostrate before the great Pandit and beg for forgiveness.

Why? Jagarakshaka chose me, *not him!*

The fires of defiance slowly melted away her fear. Even Punyamaan's anger slowly subsided, and he dismissed her as a child.

But she was a woman now. A strong woman. A woman chosen by the Protector himself!

"Maybe the scriptures don't say anything about a Pandita leading the crusade. But there won't be anything about uplifting a lowly devadasi to a Pandita either. *You* told me that exceptions can be made when the Gods themselves meddle in our matters." She crossed her arms and tilted her head up so she would be looking down at him. "Tell me, Pandit Punyamaan. Am I wrong?"

His anger returned. With it, Jagadasi felt her defiance die. Why was she so susceptible before this man? A mere look from him could frighten her just as quickly as a soft smile could make her feel nice.

"You are Jagarakshaka's chosen, and that has given you a lot of privilege, Jagadasi. Power, fame, influence. Respect beyond the dreams of anyone from your caste! Don't let it corrupt you, lest you lose what makes you pure..."

Without another word, he left her alone. The incomplete threat kept her awake that night. The only thing that Jagadasi could think of was disappointing Jagarakshaka. Would he really abandon her if she behaved poorly? Would he take away everything he had given her in these past years?

She wanted to do more. The fame she gained was infectious but short-lived. As blissful as it had felt, she had found herself growing unsatisfied. Of course, serving Jagarakshaka was a pleasure in itself, but her achievements had peaked beyond what she thought was possible.

It was time to push herself higher, wasn't it? *Give me a sign, Jagarakshaka. Please, I want to do this for you...*

Two days later, Pandit Punyamaan welcomed King

Anishtha to the Trinetra Temple. Jagadasi learned that he was a prominent Utpas King from Central Adeva. His military might had already grown to over five lakh soldiers, and would grow even more with every new kingdom he conquered.

To celebrate King Anishtha's arrival, Pandit Punyamaan decorated the entire temple with seasonal flowers of every colour. Lamps lined the path carpeted with petals. King Anishtha marched slowly, waving to the villagers and showering his good faith on them.

When he reached the foot of the temple steps, the temple attendants performed a welcoming *aarti*, cleansing his feet and offering him water and sweets. Finally, he climbed the steps to meet with Pandit Punyamaan and Jagadasi.

"Mataji," Punyamaan said, "I am honoured to present to you, Raja Anishtha of the Anishtha Kingdom. He has come to seek your blessings for his Uniting Crusade, and brings with him promises of riches to turn our little Trinetrapur into a bustling town."

King Anishtha joined his hands, "I am honoured and humbled to be in the presence of one so blessed, Mataji." He prostrated before Jagadasi and touched her feet.

She tapped his crown customarily and said, "I welcome you to the temple of Trinetra, Raja Anishtha. However, I am an insignificant nobody. The real blessings you must seek from Jagarakshaka himself."

Impressed, awed, King Anishtha rose to his feet and bowed again, "Mataji's humility is just as told. I am truly blessed to be in your presence!"

Jagadasi smiled and led him into the *garbgruha*, where Pandit Punyamaan had himself prepared for the *puja*. It took them three hours to perform the *puja*, which would ensure good luck and Jagarakshaka's blessings upon King Anishtha.

When it was completed, King Anishtha presented the Sarpanch with ten chests full of gold, silver, bronze, and jewels, a small token of thanks for Trinetrapur's hospitality. After he had personally handed the *prasad* to the villagers, he requested a private audience with Jagadasi and Pandit Punyamaan.

Once they were alone in the audience chamber, Jagadasi seated herself atop a lavish seat, while King Anishtha and Pandit Punyamaan sat on plain mats on the ground. Royalty never seemed to mind, especially since they were in the presence of a blessed god-woman.

Jagadasi knew what was expected of her, and she obliged. First, she sang hymns to praise Jagarakshaka. Then she danced without any instruments, her jewellery rattling and clinking in a rhythm musical enough. Lastly, she sat and narrated a story of Jagarakshaka's greatness. The entire performance took over an hour, at the end of which, King Anishtha praised her devotion and offered her a gold ring studded with diamonds and rubies.

Graciously, Jagadasi accepted the offering and sat back in her seat, exhausted from the performance, and eager to hear King Anishtha's request.

"Speak freely, Raja Anishtha," Pandit Punyamaan said, "What is it that you wished to ask of us?"

King Anishtha hesitated, "I-I had one request, Panditji, Mataji. I don't know if it will be possible, but I would be a fool not to attempt asking."

"Speak your mind, Raja Anishtha."

He nodded and joined his hands, "You see, my spiritual advisor, Baba Deora has unfortunately contracted a fatal disease, rendering him unable to accompany me on my crusade. Without him, my retinue lacks a place for one enlightened in the ways of *dharma*." He sat up just a bit straighter and asked Jagadasi, "Mataji, would you be willing to be my advisor?"

Jagadasi's heart skipped a beat. Despite herself, she smiled. "You want me to accompany you on the Uniting Crusade?"

"Yes, Mataji. With one such as you by my side, I would—"

"Impossible," Pandit Punyamaan interjected. "Mataji's love and devotion is to the Trinetra idol. If you take her away from here, you risk taking away this place's good fortunes. What if Jagarakshaka does not agree with her leaving?"

"I don't think Jagarakshaka will mind," Jagadasi frowned, "I cleansed this temple in his name. I have brought prosperity beyond imagination to this village. I have earned my freedom."

"Freedom?" Raja Anishtha's expression became stiff. "Are you under any pressure, Mataji?"

"No, that's not what I meant! I mean..."

"No matter how enlightened she gets, Raja Anishtha, she is still just an eighteen-year-old girl. She is allowed her little transgressions. Please," Pandit Punyamaan joined his hands, "I apologise on her behalf."

"So, now I'm just a girl?" Jagadasi's tone was rude and offended, "You just want me enslaved here, don't you?" It was all starting to make sense. His arrival was what triggered all the changes. Why hadn't Jagadasi seen this sooner?

Pandit Punyamaan's expression went dark. "I apologise if I have overstepped, Mataji. But—"

"SHUT UP!" she shouted, remembering the night she had slaughtered everyone. She assumed that expression of being possessed, letting her arms stiffen and voice grow heavy. She jumped out of her seat and began screaming, "Rarararararararararara! You don't want me to leave, do you Punyamaan? But Jagarakshaka has—"

Pandit Punyamaan slapped her hard. Jagadasi fell to the floor and lay there petrified. Behind her, she heard Pandit Punyamaan shuffle before saying softly, "I am embarrassed, Raja Anishtha, but this is... the real reason s-she cannot accompany you." For once, his speech sounded incoherent.

"I don't understand..."

"She is *blessed* by Jagarakshaka."

"I see... So..."

"I would be happy to—"

"No need to explain, Pandit Punyamaan. I shall look elsewhere for an appropriate advisor. Thank you for your honesty." He got up and walked over to Jagadasi. She was too embarrassed to turn around and look. Really, she felt like her limbs had gone stiff, unable to move at her command. Tears had welled up in her eyes, ready to flow. Behind her, she heard the king say, "Thank you for your blessings, Mataji. I will make sure the temple receives a hefty donation from my treasures. I pray Jagarakshaka protects you."

Jagadasi remained pinned to the floor as Punyamaan and Anishtha exchanged some words.

"Raja Anishtha, I apologise..."

"No, no. I completely understand," King Anishtha sounded awkward.

"She cannot leave the temple, I'm afraid. However, I can—"

"No... no need to explain. I thank you for your time, Pandit Punyamaan."

"I was going to offer..."

Jagadasi heard footsteps walking away. Pandit Punyamaan sighed.

Suddenly, she felt the blood in her hands again. What was once dead flesh now came alive. She sat up, "What did you do to me!?"

"You disobeyed me!"

"LI—" her words choked in her throat. She felt a strangulation around her neck, but there were no hands on her.

Punyamaan closed the door to the chamber and walked over to her, "You foolish bitch! You have ruined everything!"

Jagadasi couldn't even voice her confusion. She just cried and struggled to breathe.

"I gave you EVERYTHING!" He leaned into her face and hissed, "Everything! You were a fucking prostitute. I made you one of Adeva's most influential Panditas! And *this* is how you repay me? You couldn't just smile and perform your devotional songs like always, could you?" He stood up straight and shook his head, "Fucking humans... offer them a finger and they'll grab the whole fucking hand." He looked at her, then waved his hand.

Air flooded her lungs and she gulped in breaths like a starving dog.

"Your gift was this temple. You could've lived to grow old and fat."

Jagadasi wept, patting her neck, trying to find what had choked her. Was it a demon? Black magic?

"*I* was supposed to join his retinue and..." he paused. He sat down next to her. Gently stroking her head as if she were his pet, he asked, "I never told you the plan, did I?"

Meekly, Jagadasi shook her head. Somehow, he was once again the sweet priest. The man who had helped her cleanse the house of Jagarakshaka. The man she trusted.

"If only you hadn't let your stupid defiant thoughts..." his voice turned angry and dark again, "I just... ARGH!" He stopped to breathe. Quicky at first, then slowly. Once his fury was contained, he turned to her and said, "Your little performance there," he waved at the fallen chair, "will cost you, Jagadasi."

A sudden urge to grab Punyamaan's feet and beg for forgiveness assaulted her. It was stronger than her need to please her parents, stronger even than her desire to worship Jagarakshaka. Unnatural, like the sense of rage that had consumed her the night she had massacred the corrupt temple workers.

That wasn't you, was it, Jagarakshaka? You didn't help me or bless me...

"I'll behave," Jagadasi muttered, "I promise I'll do everything you tell me to. I swear by Jagarakshaka."

"We'll see," Punyamaan said, starting up. His fat slowly melted away, his body transforming into a lean and fit build like you would see on a travelling priest. Jagadasi couldn't believe her eyes.

Before she could ask, he knocked her unconscious.

Jagadasi woke up with a shock. A pain in the back of her skull made itself suddenly felt. A chill stabbed at her, and she reached out to grab her sheets, only grab damp soil. She looked up and found the stars staring down at her.

Jagadasi's heart raced. *This is a nightmare.*

She looked at herself, still wearing the same outfit she had worn during her performance. What had happened?

Slowly, she remembered the meeting with King Anishtha, how she had defied Pandit Punyamaan—

"It's coming back to you, isn't it?" Punyamaan's voice sounded disappointed.

Jagadasi felt another stab of chill. "Who are you?" She scrambled to her feet and looked around, but found no one. It was a dark moonless night, just like the night she had cleansed the Trinetra temple.

"WHO ARE YOU!?" she screamed.

He appeared before her. Lean, dressed in all black. Kurta, dhoti, even his *pheta* was black. His face was shrouded in darkness. He wasn't the same man who had helped her cleanse the temple, guided her and protected her all these years. Although, he did look like a leaner, fitter version of him.

A Rakshas? A demon? "WHO ARE YOU!?"

"SILENCE!" his voice held such absolute command that Jagadasi didn't even dare breathe. The figure walked closer to her. "Pandita Jagadasi. Servant of Jagarakshaka."

She did not speak. She did not want to disobey.

"In just a few years, you've achieved more than most kings and emperors do in lifetimes. But you wouldn't know that, would you?"

Jagadasi swallowed the lump in her throat.

"Answer me. Do you know how influential you were?"

Why was he talking in the past tense? Jagadasi quickly responded, "Yes, master." Jagadasi felt an intense need to prostrate before him. She could feel his presence on her skin, his breath in her nostrils, as if he commanded the very world she lived in. Who was this man? Was this...?

"You knew, but you didn't understand... Because, if you had, you wouldn't have acted so foolish!"

She nodded. "I'm sorry, master."

"If only you had listened to me," he said, the disappointment replaced with pity.

His words sounded final. She prostrated before him, "Master, please! Don't kill me! Please! I'll do anything!"

"No, you won't!" he snapped, "Get up."

Jagadasi fell silent again. She rose to her feet, hands still joined in begging. "Master..."

"You will die tonight, Jagadasi."

There was finality in his tone. His words, his voice, sounded like absolute truth. If anyone told Jagadasi that she was to die, she would've laughed. But when this man said it, she believed him. As if he knew the future, that he had some wise insight into life itself.

A thought crossed her mind. It was wild, preposterous, but it could explain a lot. Jagadasi bowed in submission. "I accept my fate, Jagarakshaka." It had to be him. Jagarakshaka was testing her. This had to be some divine tribulation.

The man sighed heavily. "Let me tell you a secret, Jagadasi. There is no Jagarakshaka."

"But..." Was this another test?

"The Gods left, Jagadasi. Over a thousand years ago, they left."

But...

"Most of them left, that is."

Finally... a hint! Jagadasi grabbed onto that small thread and asked, "But, you never left, did you, Jagarakshaka...?"

"Don't call me that!" the man yelled at her. She held her tongue. The silence between them grew thicker. The trees didn't rustle, no breeze blew. Not a single cricket chirped that night.

"Who are you?" Jagadasi asked, "An avatar? A follower? Who?"

Without giving an answer, the man gestured for her to follow. Jagadasi obeyed without protest.

He led her through a dark forest path. There was no crowd, no *puja*, no *aarti*. As pompous as her entry into the temple had been, her exit from the world would be equally unceremonious. She felt the cold prickle her skin. Shivering, she trailed the man slowly until they reached a clearing. She realised then why she felt so cold.

They were on top of a mountain. Below her, she spotted Trinetrapur, surrounded by its many farms. In the centre of her insignificant village lay the Trinetra Temple, illuminated by festive lights.

"Your life started there," the man said pointing. "I thought I would give you this view. God's view, before taking your life."

Jagadasi's body started convulsing. Her insides felt like they were being boiled, melting away inside of her. She fell on the ground and clutched herself. She didn't want to accept it, but the man was speaking the truth. It really was the end of her life. Her body had started submitting to death.

The man walked over to her and pulled her up. "Die with dignity, at least. You ruined my plans, but I have an alternative."

Hope sparked in her heart. "Can I..."

"No," he replied, as if he had read her mind, "You have to die for it to work."

The burning inside her imploded into a void. Her flesh was cold, her heartbeat grew slow, almost non-existent. Her body was dying, and she grew conscious of it.

Now that she stood at the threshold of death, her life seemed so insignificant to her. Despite becoming a prominent spiritual leader in Adeva, her life as a powerful being had lasted all of four years. There was so much more she could've done. She could've turned her town into a city, could've been witness to a king who would finally unite Adeva...

Did I fail...? Jagadasi cleared her throat and voiced her doubts.

The man looked at her, his eyes no longer shaded by the forest. They looked dead, emotionless.

He was old. Older than he sounded. His face was clean-shaven and his eyes looked tired. This couldn't have been Jagarakshaka. *Or maybe it's him in disguise.*

"Can I ask a question?"

"I owe you that much."

"Why me?"

"Jagadasi," the man said, "You were just at the right place at the right time."

"What...?"

The man sighed and cupped her face, "You were gullible. Pure enough to believe all that crap about cleansing, but old enough that your body could actually endure the onus."

Jagadasi felt her soul shiver. This man had lied to her, but the weight of it only just hit her. This man had used her for his gains, manipulated her into acting for his benefit, and now he was abandoning her.

Just like her parents.

"I thought I could control you, but you were just a child. I underestimated your fickleness."

"I promise—"

"It's too late. Anishtha is too devout to be lied to again. He will no doubt spread word of your *madness*. Even if you return to the temple, your fame will not last forever." He crossed his arms, "I only needed you to enter Anishtha's retinue. Without that, you are nothing to me. Not alive at least..."

"How can my death benefit you? What if I run away from here?" Desperately, she continued, "I promise I'll never come back—"

"I thought of that. But I can't erase your memories. Even if you leave, it's only a matter of time before you're tempted to return." He looked straight at her, "I can't risk that. Your sudden disappearance, however, I can use."

"How?"

He showed her a cut on his wrist, "Before

bringing you here, I left a pool of blood in your chamber. They'll discover the scene either tonight or tomorrow morning. By dusk, rumours will spread about how you and I were struck dead by Jagarakshaka's wrath." He smiled wickedly, "Stupid Anishtha will take that as a sign of his prominence, and I can use that…"

"You're a demon!" Jagadasi hissed, "You used me! How could you do something like that to another human being!?"

The man shrugged.

A crow cawed somewhere in the forest.

"It is time."

"Wait!" Jagadasi squeaked through her tears, "I can—"

The man—only recently going by the name of Pandit Punyamaan—looked around him as embers of Jagadasi's remains floated into the stagnant air.

He hated sacrificing valuable pieces, but Jagadasi had to go. Now that she had vanished, he could use her memory to further his plans.

He already knew how he would position her in the pantheon of beliefs, how her story could be manipulated. The random mystique around events in her life was perfect by chance.

A god would rise from the destruction of what was to come. And when that happened, the man would be there, moving the pieces, playing the kings and emperors of Adeva like puppets.

That, however, is a different story. Jagadasi's story ends here.

This story was also published in Grimdwarf Magazine Volumes 21-23, May 2024

THE PRINCESS WHO LOVED HER MAID

Irracayam Kingdom
800 years before King Sangaar's coronation

Princess Ilava was thirteen years old when she lost her virginity to her maid, Raci.

Ilava was the princess of the Irracayam Kingdom, a tiny almost insignificant kingdom in the southern regions of Adeva. Raci was Princess Ilava's only maid since they were both five years of age. Raci was also her best friend.

As they grew up, they realised the love they shared was more than just friendship. At age eight, they had their first kiss. At age eleven, they would spend some nights in each other's embrace, not knowing why the other's presence made them feel hot in the face and wet between the legs. At thirteen, they decided to do the deed after learning about reproduction. Of course, the missing member was made up for by a wooden toy that Raci procured from the city markets.

That night, as they lay snuggled, the realisation

dawned on both of them that they were in fact in love.

"We can't," Raci wept, "I'm a low-caste servant."

"But you'll forever be mine," Ilava pleaded, "We can make it work."

"You will be married to a king!"

"I won't! I'll delay it as much as I can. And even if I am wed, you will come with me as part of my dowry!"

"And you expect to hide this all our lives?" tears ran down Raci's almond face. "We have to stop it."

"No," Ilava insisted, pulling her closer and comforting her, "We will make it work. You have my word."

"Mahamara?" Ilava asked.

"*Raja* Mahamara," her father corrected her, "Soon to be a Maharaja. They say he has the intelligence of a hundred scholars. Others claim that he is an avatar of Jagarakshaka himself!"

Any other girl would've swooned over those words, but Ila's heart didn't have place for another lover. Her expression showed it. At least her father had asked to discuss this privately with just her and the few guards around them.

King Aracan was a pacifist. Despite having trained with weapons, he had never waged war against any of his neighbours, instead using diplomacy and wit to help his kingdom thrive. this marriage proposal was no doubt another one of his peaceful schemes.

"Asma's grace!" King Aracan exclaimed, "Mahamara doesn't have a wife yet. You should consider it an honour that out of the hundreds of proposals he got, he chose you to be his first!"

Ilava could sense Raci stiffen behind her. Ilava had to uphold her promise. "But father..."

"He will keep you happy, my Ila," her father said, "He is going to unite all of Adeva! I believe he will!"

"But..." Ilava protested, "You're a king too! Why are you bowing down to *him*!?"

Her father sighed. He looked at her with his wrinkled face and heavy eyes, leaning back in his modest throne of gold and bronze. "Ilava, you know I only lift my sword for customs, not killing. Besides, my time is nearing its end. I have to think of the future, and *this* is the best prospect I can see."

Ilava's elder brother had been twenty years her senior. He died in his very first battle after he declared he would embark on a Uniting Crusade. Her father's pacifist beliefs had never let him undertake any such. King Aracan had to settle his progeny's future before it was too late.

Ilava was only seventeen, but she understood.

Yet, she had made a promise to her beloved. "I'm too young to be married!"

"Your mother and I were married at twelve! You're lucky I didn't marry you off before your first moonblood!" King Aracan shifted in his seat and looked away. He never looked her in the eyes when he had something uncomfortable to say. "I am told you've been bleeding regularly for years."

Something about her father describing her cycles made Ilava feel uncomfortable. She had lived all her life with servants and guards around her, but not once in her seventeen years had she gotten used to that reality. Only Raci's presence brought her comfort, but it also reminded her of her predicament.

"I refuse to marry that man..." Ila said, her voice not half as assertive as she would've liked.

King Aracan got up from his throne and walked over to her. He gently lifted her chin to make their eyes meet. Although his expression was firm as a rock, she saw the sorrow in his eyes. In a voice that barely masked his shame, he said, "My darling Ila, you don't have the right to refuse. And I don't have the strength."

"I will get out of this!" Ilava shouted. They were back in her chambers, just her and Raci.

"Ila!" Raci said sternly. She approached Ila and held her in her arms. Despite the sweetening of her voice, her tone was serious, "My lovely Ila. This was meant to be."

"Why!?" Ilava screamed, not caring for any eavesdroppers. "I love *you*! Not some idiot man with a fancy hat. You!"

Raci's expression remained unchanged. "Ila, that fancy hat bears the responsibility of kingdoms whole. You don't stand a chance against that." Raci kissed her cheek, "But not to worry. You will always be in my heart. Even when my soul has crossed into the afterlife, it will wait to be united with yours."

"No," Ilava stomped her feet, "You don't understand! All my life I behaved as was expected. I was the perfect daughter, the perfect princess. And *this* is how they reward me?"

"Ila—"

"I never asked for anything! I—"

"How do you expect to earn this from your father, Ila?" Raci's voice hadn't lost her sweetness. But the sternness had grown.

Ilava hated this. Raci had always been the voice of reason in her life, no matter the mischief. "I won't let you hold me back this time."

"This time?" the sweetness faded slowly, "What do you mean *this* time?"

"I've always listened to you, Raci! If it wasn't about father's feelings, then it'd be about his status, our responsibility as royals... every time it's something or the other. When can I live for *myself*?"

Raci's expression turned glum. Tears welled up in her eyes, and Ilava knew exactly why. If Raci weren't Ilava's maid, she wouldn't have had even a tenth of the choices and luxuries. And those too Raci had because Ilava *permitted* it.

Shame twisted Ilava's chest, and she looked away. "I know what you're going to say, Raci. But—"

"You knew your father would arrange for a match. That's what princesses are for, aren't they?"

"That's wrong," Ilava said, blasphemous thoughts taking root in her mind.

"That's how it's always been, and how it'll always be, Ila. The Gods are free to do as they please. The vile Rakshasas do as they please without a care for the world."

"So, it's only good to be free as a savage, or a God, because we in the middle are forever caged?"

"Yes," Raci said composing herself, "And it's stupid for you to cry over this! You knew this was going to happen one day. Besides, even I will have to take a husband one day."

The truth stabbed at Ilava's breast. "No, this can't be! I won't allow it!"

Raci pulled her closer, "That's how the world works, Ila." Raci planted a kiss with her full brown lips on Ilava's forehead, "At least you won't be married to a servant like me."

"I'd rather be a happy servant with you, than an unhappy wife of that *king*!"

Raci kissed her on the mouth again, then smiled. "He's going to be an *emperor*!"

Ilava pushed her away, "But he isn't yet! I'll kill him on our wedding night!"

Raci gently slapped at her wrist, "Stupid girl! You can't get out of it. Just do it. I'm sure he'll keep you happy."

Ilava heard the uncertainty in Raci's voice. And behind that uncertainty, she heard pain. It broke her, made her feel something she hadn't felt since the day she saw her mother die. If her mother were alive, she wouldn't have let her father marry her off like this.

"Ila!" Raci said, a delicate finger on her chin pushing her gently to look up. "We'll make it work. You said we will, and we will. You can always have me in your dowry."

Ilava remembered saying that. She hadn't realised then how insensitive her had words sounded. Maybe it was their love for each other, or the simple fact that they were lifelong friends, but Ilava never really thought of Raci as her property.

Raci was a girl, a woman with dreams and ambitions just like her. The very thought of treating her as property made Ilava wince. This wasn't fair. Not fair at all.

"Jagarakshaka will protect us, have faith in him."

Wiping away tears, Ila forced a soft insincere smile.

Raci smiled back, pretending not to notice the storm behind Ilava's eyes.

When King Mahamara entered the royal court of Irracayam, his mere presence was enough to wane the room. His stature was average, his physique athletic, but his presence filled the room like flames engulfing oiled wood.

Everyone was in awe of the man.

The velvet carpets seemed like lowly rags when his bejewelled sandals fell upon them. The rich drapes embroidered in bronze felt like loose strips of old cloth hanging about. Even the nobles within felt like insignificant insects when compared to the almost divine presence of King Mahamara.

He was welcomed with the juiciest fruits, the richest fabrics and pots of coins and gemstones. His presence made them look like worthless trinkets. But when he held them in his hands, they looked like riches. Mahamara accepted the offerings with a smile that made everyone believe that they were in his good graces.

Finally, Ilava was presented to him. After all that preceded her, she should have felt grateful when the man laid his eyes on her. However, all she could feel was disgust.

Ilava was all decked up with the finest jewels, fabrics and scents that Raci could get her hands on. Yet, she felt like a piece of meat on sale. All she could think of when she saw the man was the loss of her freedom. This would be the man she would be expected to lie with, whose children she would have to bear. And she wasn't given any say in it.

The thought of those fine arms caressing her skin should have made her blush, but all she felt was ire. Then, Mahamara's reputation and presence pulled at Ilava's heart. The moment she met his gaze, she felt her insides flutter. She had never felt this unnatural attraction towards any man before. It felt forced, as if unseen strings had latched onto her heart and were drawing them towards him.

Her feelings for Raci were much stronger though, and she fought the urge to smile. This man wasn't her beloved and never would be.

Ilava tried not to flinch as King Mahamara's eyes lingered on her body. Despite the heavy sari and jewellery, she felt naked and exposed. Her body reacted as if it wanted to bed this man, but her mind couldn't stop feeling disgusted, a confused mix of emotions swirling in her mind, precursing a headache.

When she dared to meet his gaze again, there was

intrigue in them, as if he had heard the thoughts in her mind, as if he knew her very soul and was hungry to ravish it. "I will marry her," King Mahamara declared, knowing he already had King Aracan's blessings.

No one asked for Ilava's opinion.

The pulling on her heart stopped. She was herself again and felt no attraction to the man she was now betrothed to. But the room didn't notice her distress. Everyone from the nobles to their attendants, to the guards and servants, everyone erupted in applause as if the Gods themselves had demanded it.

Ilava clenched her fist, wanting to beat everyone who celebrated her sale. Her heart threatened to pound out of her chest, but she braved herself. She wouldn't go down without a fight. She cleared her throat and croaked. But no one heard.

She pretended to clear her throat again, then shouted out loud, "I have one condition!"

The court silenced itself. Just as awestruck as everyone was when King Mahamara entered the room, everyone was shocked at Princess Ilava's nerve.

Her father immediately stepped forward to pacify the situation, but King Mahamara raised his hand. There was a playful glint in his eyes as he looked at Ilava. "Speak."

"After the wedding, I want to take my own maid with me."

King Mahamara studied Ilava's eyes, his gaze already sent a chill through her soul. She wanted to shiver but fought the urge. She gulped but stood unmoved.

Mahamara looked past Ilava, studying Raci as if she too were a potential bride. After little thought, Mahamara casually replied. "No."

King Aracan had never slapped his daughter, which was why Ilava's cheek burned more with shock than pain.

Ilava spent the next hour listening to her father scold her, tears drenching her blouse and sari. He didn't care that her hair was dishevelled, or that her delicate jewellery broke off. When he left, he left her with a death threat. *Don't you dare shame me, or I will kill you with my own hands.*

It echoed in her ears and stabbed at her skull. How could her own father say something so vile? This wasn't the doting father who had raised her, this was a bad man from folk tales who used his daughter as a bargaining chip in political games. Had her father really stooped that low?

"Because he is also a king, Ila!" Raci comforted her, "He has his duties, and so do you."

"And he couldn't give me just this one wish? Is saving face more important than his own daughter?"

"To a king, yes." Raci frowned.

"It's all my fault! I shouldn't have spoken up."

"Why did you?"

"Because I promised you! I wanted to make sure I kept that promise."

Raci frowned. "I can understand."

"I hate this world. I wish I could just... run away!"

"Ila, we're not kids anymore." She cupped her face and wiped away the tears with her thumb. "Sacrifice is part of life."

"Then let me sacrifice my life! I will not marry that vile man!"

"Vile? Did you not see him? It's as if the very heavens hover about him! I'm sure he will unite Adeva. Mark my words, Ila." Raci's tone when speaking about Mahamara was eerily similar to the way she spoke about Ilava. Was she lusting after that man? Had he managed to charm her with a mere gaze? Just the thought of it was infuriating.

"I don't care if he's Jagarakshaka himself! I will not marry him!" Ilava pulled herself away and rose to her feet. "Why must *I* sacrifice anything at all?"

"Because that's what is expected of you," Raci said, "You're a princess. You can't inherit anything." Raci rose to her feet, "You know that, Ila. Don't act foolish."

"No," Ila stomped her feet. "I'd rather die."

"You'd leave me alone?" Raci frowned. Tears welled but she held them back. "I'd rather you live a life away from me than give up your life for me. I won't be able to live with myself."

Ilava turned away, not having the courage to look at Raci.

Yet, Raci continued, "If you marry and go, I'll still be able to live a happy life here in the palace. As your personal maid, I've received enough favour from your father." Raci held Ilava and turned her around. "But if something were to happen to you, I'll have to take part of the blame. I'll either be punished, or condemned. Would you let me suffer like that? Would your soul find peace knowing I was suffering?

"And your father? Imagine the shame, the dishonour! Yours is already a small kingdom. This marriage is his chance to give you a better life. Think about it, Ilava."

Ilava realised she too was weeping. She grabbed Raci and hugged her tightly, and the two wept on each other's shoulders.

By the time their tears were dry, Ilava had a plan.

The wedding procession was the grandest,

loudest event in two hundred years. King Mahamara's *baraat* was led by tigers, elephants, rhinos and other exotic animals, with peacocks flying above, all controlled by *Pashupathis* decked in gold and jewels. Behind them was a retinue of horses, followed by the groom riding a gold-laden mare. People danced and celebrated around him in the *baraat*, dressed in the finest clothes they could afford. They cheered their lungs dry, as priests chanted praises and hymns to the Gods. Some even begged the Gods to return and witness the ostentation.

When King Mahamara stepped down from his mare and entered the royal palace, his presence had the opposite effect of his previous visit. The velvet carpets seemed to soften at his footfalls. The flowers and petals offered to him seemed to bloom brighter, letting out stronger fragrances of peace and joy.

When Mahamara entered the royal court—which had now been transformed into a majestic *mandap*—the lanterns seemed to burn brighter. The air was filled with deafening cheers as he was seated on his nuptial *patda*. He sat with his back straight, the diamonds and jewels on his plush robes glimmering in the lantern light.

The auspicious hour finally arrived, and his bride was brought to him. Decked in a pure white silk sari, embroidered with gold thread and diamonds, that matched the opulence of her necklaces, bangles and rings. As custom had it, her face was covered with her *pallu*, only to be lifted by her husband on their nuptial bed. To Mahamara's surprise, his bride did not fight or protest. She obeyed the priest's instructions with astute servility.

Mahamara was pleased to have an obedient wife.

As the doors to his chambers were shut, Mahamara

settled into his bed, arousal making him restless. It had been quite some time since he had bedded a princess.

King Mahamara watched his new bride approach with nervous steps, a golden plate in her hands that held a large copper tumbler of honeyed milk. He accepted the glass and downed the milk, knowing he could proceed with his other duties.

"Come, sit," he commanded.

She obeyed.

He placed his hand on hers. She flinched. He reached out and grabbed it anyway, "We're married now. No need to be scared." He slid closer to her. "I promise to give you the world. I will unite Adeva, and you will rule over all of it. My queen. My beloved." He kissed her through the pallu, the tease of her almond-shaped face igniting flames of desire in his loins. He expected her to shudder, expected her to go breathless as his presence aroused her wildest passions.

Instead, all he heard from her was a soft sniff.

"Ilava!" his voice melted into consideration, "Why do you weep? I will not hurt you." He slid slightly away, "If you want to wait, we can. But we must lie together tonight. It is an auspicious time. For all you know, we might even conceive!"

That made her weep even more.

Mahamara frowned. The room turned brighter as he rose to his feet. His nuptial night was not going as expected, and he was not in the mood to bed a courtesan. "I can understand if you feel this is forced. But one day, you will realise that your father did the right thing. Now come," he held her *pallu*, ready to unveil her beauty.

Her hands grabbed his tightly, stopping him.

The candles flickered ominously. Mahamara's voice was frigid. "What is the meaning of this? You insolent woman!"

With the strength of a bull, he ripped the *pallu* off. What he saw sent a bubbling rage through his gut. The candles extinguished, violent winds buffeting the heavy curtains, threatening to wreck the chamber and its contents.

His wife wept, seeing the murder in Mahamara's eyes. She saw his fists clenched, ready to strike. She fell to her knees. "Forgive me, my king. I..."

Mahamara kicked her hard across the face. He made sure to hold back so she would only be knocked out. He saw her sprawled on the floor, his wife, a low-caste maid.

Mahamara kicked the doors, and they flew off their hinges. He stormed towards King Aracan's quarters, trying his best not to wreck the palace in his rage. After all, this was his palace now. He had earned it as dowry.

His footfalls sounded like tremors of an impending earthquake. Soldiers and guards jumped out of his way to avoid getting trampled. When he reached his *father-in-law's* chambers, he didn't bother to knock. He kicked so hard at the thick doors that they flew back and crashed against the far-off wall.

Luckily, King Aracan's bed was not in the path of the crash. The old king jumped, pushing away the naked courtesan from him. He barely had time to cover himself before Mahamara screamed.

"WHAT IS THE MEANING OF THIS?"

Confused, King Aracan pulled the blankets about him. "What are you saying, my son?" Fear painted his face white as if he had been given the death sentence.

Mahamara stepped forward, "Don't call me son, you scheming..."

"It's not his fault," a woman's voice cut him.

Mahamara turned and saw a woman at the door. She was draped in a black sari, covered by a black shawl. No ornaments adorned her neck, no bangles, no earrings. It took him a moment to recognise the woman he was supposed to have married.

"It was all me," she said, the defiance clear in her voice. There was no shame on her face.

Mahamara clenched his teeth. He stepped forward, ready to slap Ilava. She threw back her shawl and pulled out a long knife.

Ilava spat at his feet. "Strike me, and you will bleed. I don't care if people think you're a godsend. You could be Jagarakshaka reincarnate and I'd still not let you touch me!"

Mahamara, unconcerned, stepped forward and pulled the knife away from her. Without flinching, he squeezed his hand and the knife shattered like a clay toy. His hand was unhurt. "Explain yourself. NOW!"

"Not here," King Aracan said, finally draping a dhoti around his waist, "Please."

The door was shut. King Mahamara watched with crossed arms as King Aracan beat his daughter for the abominable sin she had committed.

"It's unnatural!" he shouted, "Where did I falter!?"

Slap.

"Your mother must be beating herself in the afterlife for birthing you!"

Slap.

"How could you do this?"

Slap.

"Have you no shame?"

At this point, Ilava had lost count of how many times her father had slapped her. She had grown numb to the pain. She didn't even care if there were permanent marks on her perfect skin, anything that would break off her marriage with Mahamara was worth enduring.

The doors opened, and the bride—now unkempt from her interrogation—was brought in. She was stripped of her jewels and riches, only a sari left on her body to preserve her modesty.

"This was the whore who ensnared you?" King Aracan bellowed. Ilava wasn't used to such language from her father. She did not respond. King Aracan picked up a fruit knife. "I'll kill her!"

Ilava jolted upright as she saw her father dart towards her beloved. "NO!!!"

Her father readied to stab. Raci flinched and blocked herself with her arms.

The knife never reached her. Mahamara stepped between them.

King Aracan, pale and shocked, "What are you doing?"

"You want her dead?" Mahamara asked, "Asma's grace! She is my wife."

King Aracan dropped the knife. "But…"

"What's done cannot be undone," Mahamara shook his head, then pointed to Ilava. "This is your daughter's doing!" His accusing finger was like a spearpoint ready to stab her.

At that moment, Ilava understood the deep repercussions of her actions. Mahamara's words shook her soul. She had been so blinded by her love and rage that she had acted poorly.

King Aracan was trembling now. "But…"

"What's done is done," Mahamara said, "You gave away your kingdom in dowry," he gestured to Raci with a disgusted look, "For a low-caste maid."

"But…"

"SILENCE!" Mahamara screamed. King Aracan

fell to his knees. It was as if Mahamara's voice had stabbed the servility into him.

Ilava's heart broke when her father finally broke down. He hid his face out of shame and wept like a little child.

"You!" Mahamara screamed at her, "You really thought you could get away with this?"

His voice sent shivers down her spine. She trembled at his very gaze.

"What for?" Mahamara spread his arms, "You were willing to give all this up," he pointed to Raci, "For *this*? Are you insane?"

His voice stopped Ilava from responding. She looked at her father only to see a defeated man. She looked back at Mahamara, the man who was supposed to unite Adeva, a godsend, an avatar of God, a hero... a puny selfish man.

"You see a low-caste maid," Ilava croaked, "I see the love of my life." She rose to her feet, challenging Mahamara's glare with her own. "You see a low-caste maid. I see a human being."

"The Gods themselves have laid the foundation for our society, girl. To challenge them is sin."

"It is a stupid system. Inhumane." Ilava clenched her jaw, trying her best not to curse the Gods.

Her face was numb, her body covered in bruises, but nothing could stop her now. If she was to die, let her die a proud woman. "Kill me if you want. There is nothing you can do to stop me from loving her."

Mahamara's anger didn't recede, but a new sensation blinked into his eyes. "So, you're one of those idealists who thinks the world should treat everyone equally, is it? Lost, mind rotted by tales of perfect worlds? That's not how this world functions, girl."

Ilava felt a shiver run down her spine. She didn't know what this man was capable of, but she had already said too much to back down.

"Let her go," Raci begged, "Please." She fell to Mahamara's feet, "I will do anything, just don't hurt my Ila."

Mahamara looked from Raci to Ilava. Ilava saw wonder in his eyes. Fascination. "You two," he pointed to them one at a time, "would give your life for the other?"

Raci looked up. Ilava nodded. Raci imitated her.

"Get up." Raci obeyed. "You," he said to Raci, "are now my wife. You won't be the first low-caste woman to enter my bed, but you won't father any heirs. Even if you do, they will never have any real claim to my kingdom."

Raci looked to Ilava, all confused and frightened.

"King Aracan," his voice was pitiful, "It is a shame that Asma's grace was short-lived for you. I pray the Creator has written of better days in your old age. The Protector, however, has blessed me and I vow to extend that to you. You will continue to live a comfortable life under my protection. After all, it isn't every day that a king gives up his kingdom in dowry for a lowly maid." A booming laughter echoed in the air.

Infectious, it tickled the bones of the guards and servants around them. Even King Aracan forced a chuckle, not wanting to insult the great King Mahamara's *kindness*. Everyone laughed, save for Ilava and Raci. It was cruel. It was unjust.

It was what it was. Ilava held back tears, bracing herself to hear her punishment.

Mahamara ignored her and looked to Raci, "We have made a vow before the Gods, and we must hold up our end." Before Raci could reply, Mahamara turned to Ilava, "And you. You wanted your maid so badly that you gave up your stake at being a queen? You're the stupidest woman I've ever met. And I know just the way to punish you." Mahamara offered them his hands.

Ilava looked to her father, who was still kneeling down. He averted his gaze, seemingly having disowned his daughter.

Ilava looked at Mahamara and thought she understood what he was saying. Hesitantly, she took his hand.

However, it was not what she had expected.

The next day, a grand procession was held in honour of the newlyweds. The opulence of this celebration matched Mahamara's *baraat*. Except this time, there were no exotic animals, no birds, no mares. Dancers and artisans performed for the cheering public, as soldiers marched in perfect synchronisation.

In the middle of the procession was a grand chariot upon which stood Mahamara, dressed in clothes as fine and rich as his wedding attire. Next to him, stood his wife, matching his opulence. The new queen of his kingdom, who would one day become queen of Adeva.

Behind their chariot was their retinue of servants, walking on foot. Among those servants was the queen's personal maid, Ilava.

Mahamara's punishment was a blessing to Ilava and Raci. He vowed never to even touch either woman. Their punishment was being denied his godly body.

To add salt to their wounds, Mahamara thought he could humiliate Ilava by making her Raci's servant. But, being a maid was a small price to pay for being with her beloved for the rest of their lives.

Everyone in the procession beamed with happiness, but none as purely as Ilava.

Over the years, this tale would take on a very

romantic connotation. Lovers across Adeva would celebrate the romance between the Princess and her servant. Everyone would speak of Mahamara's generosity and the power of Raci and Ilava's love. However, in those tales, Raci's birth would be rewritten from being a low-caste nobody to being the bastard son of a defeated king. Yes, both her low birth and her gender were changed for what society deemed proper.

History is full of lies, written by the people in power to make them seem better, and this was one such tale. But, Raci and Ilava lived happy enough lives. They didn't care what the world would remember them as. They were happy to be with each other, to grow old together, and to have their love last a whole lifetime, and beyond.

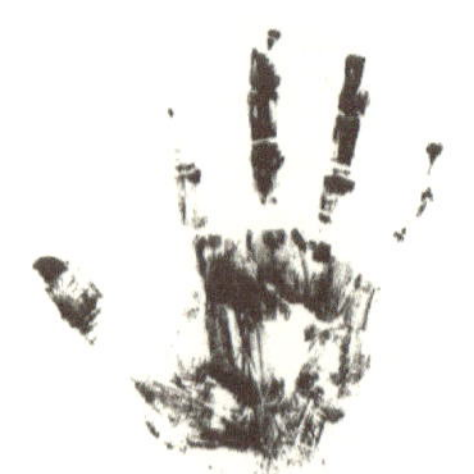

DACOIT, SON OF A NOBLE

*Somewhere in Central Utpas,
A few years before King Ina's coronation*

Bhola was thirteen years old when he watched his father die. He wanted to scream his lungs out, but his uncle covered his mouth. They hid in the shadows, witnessing the slaughter.

Roaring flames engulfed their palace. His father's headless body convulsed on the marble floor.

"The *zamindar* is dead!" the invaders declared, applauding the murder. These nightmarish images would haunt Bhola for the rest of his life.

"Secret passage next to the Jagarakshaka idol... use it and run Bhola," his uncle whispered hastily, hand pressed on Bhola's mouth, "But stay in the shadows. Make sure they don't catch you."

Bhola pulled his uncle's hand away, "Chachu..." he said between short breaths, "what about... Baba...?"

"He's dead!" Chachu hissed, "You have to keep living. You'll have your revenge, I promise!"

"But…"

"Run to the hills, I will find you!" saying that, his uncle let go. Not knowing what else he could do, Bhola ran. He made his way towards the secret passage.

It wasn't a straight path, debris and dead bodies scattered everywhere he stepped.

Every time he hid, he saw hideous scenes of bloodshed. Soldiers clad in brown and black had mercilessly slaughtered everyone. He didn't know what was happening, but now was not the time to think.

He found the Jagarakshaka idol and sneaked into the storage chamber where the passage was hidden. Once inside, the cold darkness embraced him. He kept touching the wall, walking briskly. His little teenage heart threatened to give out.

Bhola had to stop and remind himself to breathe. If they found him now, he'd be killed like Baba. Or worse.

He had to run. And he did.

Everyone was dead. His father lay headless in one of the rooms; he didn't remember which one. He didn't even know where his mother and sister were. He considered returning for them. But then he decided Chachu would take care of it. He trusted Chachu's word. He ran.

Outside the palace, the situation wasn't much different. Their little city lay bare and open to the raiders. People cut down like livestock littered the streets. Burning houses shed an ominous light on the violence that occupied the night.

Bhola ran. Ignoring the pain of everyone in their little city, he ran.

And hid.

And ran.

And hid.

He was scared out of his wits. The only thing keeping him going was Chachu's promise. His arms and legs had grown weary. His lungs burned with fatigue, weakened by the black smoke from his burning home.

Despite everything he ran.

Bhola had to survive. He had to avenge his family, even if it meant giving everything up.

In the distance, Bhola saw the smoke rising to the stars. There was an amber glow around his city. The life he had known now burned to ashes. He could never return.

Never.

Bhola found a tree which he climbed up. Ants and spiders crawled about him, but those creepy insects were welcome friends compared to the ruthless soldiers that were decimating his life.

Where are you, Chachu?

Bhola felt something cold touch him, and he immediately froze. *Idiot.*

A snake slithered up his leg. He felt its cold weight on his thighs. His heart raced, almost audibly.

Calm down, Bhola. It won't do anything.

Bhola had seen snakes before. He had even held snakes under supervision. He hoped it wasn't a venomous snake. It would be impossible to confirm given his position. How was he to check the snake's scales in the dark?

He swallowed his spit, realising then how dry his throat was. His leg threatened to shake, his mind draining itself to keep them steady.

Calm down. Calm down.

The snake slithered onto his back and fell to the side. Immediately the side of his torso felt pin prickles.

It's not a bite. It's just you. Calm down. Think

what Baba would do. Think what Chachu would do.

The snake slowly slithered from his torso towards his hands. The moment it climbed on, Bhola held his breath. *Jagarakshaka, please protect me.*

The snake slithered onto his head, and Bhola shut his eyes tightly. *Please, Jagarakshaka. Praise be upon you. Please protect me.*

Aum Jai Jagarakshaka!

Aum Jai Jagarakshaka!

Bhola continued to chant praises to the Protector, but the snake seemed to have found a perfect spot to rest. It stayed there, its cold scaly form on Bhola's head.

Bhola had to control himself. He wondered what bad karma he had incurred in his past life for him to be suffering so.

And then Bhola thought that maybe the Protector had sent this snake. To cool him down after the heat of flight. Maybe this was the Protector's sign to him that everything would be okay.

The Gods worked in mysterious ways. The snake wasn't a bad omen. Bhola believed it to be true, the thought comforting him.

Bhola's heart slowed down, pumping normally. His breathing steadied too. He actually found the snake's presence reassuring, as if Jagarakshaka or Durajaya were personally making sure he was safe.

That's it! Durajaya!

The Destroyer was known to care for all animals, including snakes. It was *his* sign.

A sign from two of the triumvirate. Jagarakshaka wanted to protect him. Durajaya wanted to remind him that he had to destroy his enemies.

The thoughts occupied Bhola's mind, distracting him from the pain and suffering of that night.

He didn't even realise when he drifted off to

sleep.

Bhola awoke to the crunching noise of footsteps. They were at a distance, but the night was silent and the presence of people heavy.

Bhola started up and almost lost balance. He reminded himself that he was on a tree branch and gripped it tighter. He couldn't feel the snake's touch or presence around him.

Bhola held his breath, hoping that would keep him steady, but that was the very moment an itch burnt on his legs. The ants and spiders had probably gnawed at his flesh when he slept.

Bhola felt his insides scream. Parts of his flesh felt like they were on fire. But he kept silent, trying to identify the distant forms that approached him.

Idiot, couldn't you have climbed a tree that was further away from the hill's trail?

As they came closer, Bhola noticed a blade glint in the moonlight. The sudden realisation of being unarmed hit him like an enemy's arrow. The figures treading the hill's trail were cautious, he could tell from their movements.

As they neared, he heard hushed voices. Familiar voices.

"Chachu!" he called out.

Weapons raised, they halted.

"Bhola?" Chachu's voice was guarded.

Bhola slid down the tree and presented himself to the group. It took Chachu less than a heartbeat to rush to his nephew and embrace him tightly.

This was the first time Bhola had seen any man in his family cry real tears.

"Bhola... my nephew! Jagarakshaka has kept you safe! Praise be upon him!"

Chachu's embrace suddenly reminded Bhola of the vice grip he had held Bhola in when his father was being killed. Flashes of the beheading. The heat. The screams. The chaos.

Bhola pushed himself free, screaming in horror.

Startled, Chachu took a step back. "Bhola?"

Bhola couldn't contain himself. He wept. He let his broken heart finally feel the pain of his loss.

It gushed like a full river in the middle of a thunderstorm, deep and dominant enough to drown even elephants.

Chachu pulled him closer, caressing him, "Weep, boy. Weep."

Bhola clutched onto Chachu's clothes, dug his face deep into his chest and let his tears soak them.

"Weep all you want tonight, boy," Chachu said, "You won't get another chance."

When Bhola awoke the next morning, he hoped it was all a nightmare.

He was wrong.

Their city was too far away for them to smell the destruction, but the residual smoke lingered on the horizon. Bhola was still haunted by flashes of the night. He had learned not to react to them.

They had made a makeshift camp in the hills. There wasn't any river nearby, so they had to be frugal about water.

When it was time to break their fast, Bhola was given just a handful of berries.

"We aren't nobles anymore, Bhola," Chachu broke the news. "We can't go back."

Bhola did not question. He was old enough to know when to shut up. If peace had prevailed, he would have started helping his father with his duties soon. However, the enemy's raid had ruined everything.

"Who was that, Chachu?"

Chachu frowned. Eyes reddening with anger.

"Are you deaf or are you dumb?"

"What do you mean...?"

"Didn't you pay attention when your Baba spoke at court?"

Bhola grew nervous. His uncle rarely scolded him like this.

Chachu's expression reminded him of the soldiers screaming death. "ANSWER ME!"

"NO!" Bhola screamed back, "Baba didn't tell me anything!" Tears lined his eyes.

He could tell that Chachu wanted to scream, but he held himself back. He gathered his anger and spat it out on the side. "Your mother has made you soft, boy. We need to change that." He chewed on that for a while, then shouted to a nearby guard—one of only five that had managed to escape. "Rana! Come here."

Rana was a big man, not muscular but imposing nonetheless. He was a former *Pehlwan* who had saved Chachu's life during a hunt. Since then, Rana had served as Chachu's personal bodyguard and right hand. "Yes, *sahib*?"

Chachu got up, "Tell the boy everything about the kings and kingdoms of Adeva." Saying that he walked away to tend to other matters.

Rana took Bhola to the side and spent the next hour explaining the politics of Adeva.

"Anandananta?" Bhola asked.

Rana nodded, "They call him Raja Ananda. He was an upper-caste noble who rose to prominence after killing his king, that vile scum." Rana muttered a curse. "He's undertaken the Uniting Crusade."

"Just like Raja Durana," Bhola added, hoping to sound knowledgeable.

"Raja Durana doesn't have the numbers that Ananda has."

Bhola frowned. That's why it had been so easy for Ananda's soldiers to sack their city overnight.

"A few months back, he sent us a proposal to surrender peacefully. Surrendering would mean leaving Raja Durana's kingdom open for assault. Care to guess what your father might have said?"

Baba wasn't a king, just a *zamindar*. He took good care of their city and neighbouring villages, earning a lot of favour from Raja Durana for his loyalty and righteous conduct. Bhola said, "He must've refused."

Rana nodded, "Your father's loyalty cost us everything, boy."

Bhola frowned. "What do we do now?"

Rana unsheathed his sword and handed it over. "Now we train."

Bhola looked at the blade suspiciously, "Swordplay?"

Rana shook his head. "Your family's wealth no longer exists. You don't have rich or powerful relatives to help us." He proffered the sword, hilt first this time, "We're on our own."

Bhola's eyes narrowed. "Raja Durana…"

Chachu shouted, returning, "He's a coward, that fat asshole. Ananda has made an example of us," he stood next to Rana, "That's enough to make Durana surrender."

Bhola looked at the sword again, then accepted it. It was heavier than the ones he had practised with. "What will we do?" he asked Rana.

Rana looked to Chachu before answering, "Dacoity."

The plains were lush that monsoon. The grass almost glowed green as it gently swayed along the trader roads. Dew clung to their blades, just as blood clung to the dacoits' weapons.

Beside the road, a chariot lay abandoned. Dead guards with fatal wounds lay around it. The merchant couple that owned the chariot knelt at the dacoit's feet, begging for mercy.

The couple wore matching green outfits. He wore a peacock green silk kurta with gold leaf embroidery in the Limat style. She wore a matching nine-yard silk sari with gold and silver thread borders. Their necks were decked in gold, jewels, and a noose whose other end lay in the hands of a menacing-looking man wearing a black vest, maroon pyjamas and a black turban.

"You can either tell us what more riches you're hiding, or we can rip your chariot apart and find them ourselves." This from another dacoit.

The portly man with a balding pate begged with joined hands, "I gave you all we had."

"What about your ornaments?" a third one asked, pointing his dagger at their throats, "You two fatsos look like you already ate a kingdom's worth."

The gang laughed, everyone except their Sardar. He had a menacing look to him, a serpent tattoo coiling around his right hand. He was the only man wearing a maroon turban. He raised his muscular hand and shouted, "Silence! What are you, jesters? Just get it over with."

The merchant recognised the leader and immediately diverted his attention to him, "Sardar! Please! We're harmless. We don't even have bodyguards anymore!" They lay dead around their chariot. "You've taken our chests." Stacked behind the Sardar. "At least spare us these ornaments!" he joined his hands to beg, "They're family heirlooms."

The Sardar's expression was stonelike. "Rana."
He replied, "Yes, Sardar?"

"If they don't surrender their ornaments, hack off their heads and retrieve the gold."

Rana gave a menacing grin, "Gladly, Sardar."

"And don't forget their threads. They look bloody pricy."

The Sardar didn't bother paying attention to the merchants' pleas. He knew they'd oblige.

"You shouldn't have stripped the woman," Chachu reprimanded, "We aren't that kind of gang." The flames of their cookfire cast dancing shadows on his face. Night painted the skies a dark purple, embroidered with twinkling stars and a half-moon with a dull glow. Dark clouds threatened to shower the world again that night.

"How does it matter?" Bhola spat out a bone into the fire, then retorted, "We were harmless merchants too. Did that save my mother? My sister? Can you guarantee they died a quick death?"

Chachu looked away from Bhola, turning his attention to the piece of mutton in his hand.

Bhola scoffed. "At least we didn't rape the bitch. If they're lucky, no one will harm them." Even he knew that was a stretch. Their chariot would likely be caught by another gang, and seeing an almost naked woman without guards was enough motivation for them to have their way. "Anyway, that couple came from Nishanata, didn't they? Ananda's capital. If I could..."

"Are you listening to yourself?" Chachu snapped, dropping his plate to the ground. Expression gaunt, Chachu got up and walked away.

Chachu had spent the last four years making a dreadful dacoit out of Bhola. What started as survival ended up making Bhola a dark man with a darker reputation. "You made me, Chachu!" Bhola shouted after him, "This is who I am now!"

Chachu did not respond.

Bhola returned to his meat, chewing on dark thoughts. His eyes looked to the flames, flashes of his father's death still haunting him. However, they didn't frighten him anymore. If anything, those flames roiled something within his soul. Burnt it dark. Vengeance had become his life's goal, which was why his gang targeted traders and convoys going to and from the Ananta Kingdom.

"You know, Bhola," Rana said, chewing audibly, "People get jumpy when you start attacking their women." He ripped off a huge chunk straight off the bone and continued to chew. "It's not like you haven't attracted enough attention."

Bhola didn't take his eyes off the flames, "Good."

After dinner, Bhola walked over to the edge of the camp. The darkness that he once feared was now a welcoming friend. The fires behind were beginning to die down.

Bhola found a spot, squatted and pissed carefully. He always found relieving himself a major inconvenience as a dacoit. No matter how much his body had grown accustomed to the harsh life, his mind still hated it. Although a negligible complaint, it added to his unending list of reasons to seek revenge.

A twig snapped.

Bhola grew alert. He slowly reached for the dagger in his belt.

"Sardar Bhola?" a soft voice called out.

Bhola did not respond. He tried to gauge his surroundings, hand reaching for a dagger strapped to his ankle.

"I wish I had found you in a better position."

Bhola found the voice's location and threw the dagger at the stranger standing behind him.

The stranger caught the dagger. By the hilt.

Bhola grew tense. He was open and vulnerable.

"Put your dick back in and let's talk."

"Why?"

"Because," the stranger lowered the dagger, "I have some information for you."

"Keep talking," Bhola said, rising up slowly.

"I won't attack you," the stranger said. In a flash, Bhola's dagger lodged itself in the soil between his legs. "Unless you make me."

Bhola's throat went dry. This was a formidable foe. Was he one of Ananda's? An assassin?

The stranger began, "You have sworn vengeance on Raja Ananda. Well," he paused briefly, "I might as well say *Maharaja* Ananda. Let's not forget his success with the Uniting Crusade."

Was Ananda an emperor now? The thought made Bhola grimace. "Are you one of his?"

The stranger stepped closer. The dull moonlight revealed a bushy beard and saintly robes. A *priest*?

"Who are you?"

"A messenger," the stranger said, "The Gods left Adeva a thousand years ago, but they still take a keen interest in its happenings." The mere mention of the Gods seemed to still the air. The clouds drifting in the sky halted in position. The stars stopped twinkling. Bhola's breathing slowed down, urging him to kneel to this stranger.

What is happening?

The stranger pointed to Bhola's serpent tattoo, "You believe me, right?"

Bhola looked at his arm, the tattoo barely visible in the moonlight. It had given him strength over the years. The Gods themselves had sent him a sign, both the Protector and the Destroyer. He clenched his fist and looked at the stranger.

Normally, Bhola would demand an explanation.

But with this stranger, his instincts betrayed him. This wasn't an ordinary man. This wasn't even an extraordinary king. This was a messenger of the Gods, and his presence imposed itself on Bhola.

The stranger finally spoke, "Ananda is one *puja* away from becoming a Maharaja."

The words rang in Bhola's mind like war drums. His guts twisted inside.

The stranger growled, "He must fail."

Bhola's tongue loosened, finally granting him speech. Was it the stranger's doing? "Where?" his voice croaked.

The stranger crossed his arms. "You will learn of the time and location from another dacoit. You must join forces with him."

Bhola considered it. Dacoits rarely joined forces, unless circumstances demanded it. "Who?"

"Sauraga," the stranger said.

Sauraga was another dacoit like Bhola. A noble forced into a life of crime after Ananda had conquered his lands.

Maybe this really was divine intervention. The Gods worked in mysterious ways. For once, a wronged dacoit would get a chance at claiming justice. *Two* wronged dacoits. "I will do it," Bhola declared, "I will stop that bastard Ananda."

The stranger stepped closer and cupped Bhola's face. Bhola's body froze. He couldn't even blink of his own volition.

"The fate of Adeva depends on you, Bhola," the stranger said. His hands started to glow. Dim at first. Then blinding.

A flash slapped Bhola in the face. As it faded, the stranger was nowhere in sight. The world returned to normalcy. The clouds drifted again. The stars twinkled. And Bhola lay on the ground, wondering who the stranger was.

A week passed before Bhola received word from Sauraga's gang. They wanted to meet.

Bhola readily accepted despite Chachu's protests. He didn't care about the risks. All he wanted was vengeance.

Bhola's gang had to travel for two days outside their territories into neutral ground.

On the night of their meeting, they reached the predetermined location. Sauraga's gang of dacoits was already there feasting on stolen sheep. Three cookfires indicated they were larger in numbers, but they weren't as infamous as Bhola's gang.

"That's the one?" Chachu asked.

"Yes," Rana replied, "Just like us, apparently."

"Are you sure about this, Bhola?" Chachu asked.

Bhola simply grunted.

Chachu sighed, then said, "Let me do the talking."

Bhola didn't protest. It would be better that way.

The night sky had a rotten orange tint to it. It reminded Bhola of the amber glow above his burning city.

Chachu led his gang—now comprising twenty dacoits—towards the larger gang that Bhola hoped he could command.

When the other dacoits saw them approaching, their Sardar came forth to greet them.

"Sardar Bhola!" he shouted without a care, his voice deep and commanding. "Welcome to our camp!"

"Sardar Sauraga," Chachu shouted, "We accept your gracious welcome!"

The sound of noble etiquette coming from the dacoits was quite off-putting. Bhola hadn't heard such politesse too often in four years.

"You must be Bhola's Chachu," Sauraga said joining his hands, "May Jagarakshaka protect you."

"And you, Sardar," Chachu joined his hands, "My nephew, Sardar Bhola."

Bhola joined his hands and faked a smile, trying to gauge the man. Sauraga was stout, much like the merchant they'd robbed a week before. However, Sauraga's notoriety was unquestioned.

Sauraga wore his vest unbuttoned, letting the world see his scar-laden belly. His chest was wide, and his arms thick. Despite his heavy appearance, there was a certain grace to his movements. Probably because he had been a trained musician and dancer before becoming a dacoit.

"The Bhoomipadh Household," Sardar Sauraga said as his men served food, "was renowned for creating a fusion between the Bhoomivaani School of Music and the Jagapadha School of Dance. It was a revolutionary art form. My father spent his life perfecting two full art forms before making that fusion, and then passed it on to us!"

"May Jagarakshaka protect his soul," Chachu added, "There were none like the Bhoomipadh Household!"

"Indeed," Sardar Sauraga nodded, trailing a scar on his belly with a gnarled finger, "That vile Ananda ruined everything. His barbaric actions have thrown the arts a few years behind! Decades maybe!"

Bhola grunted in agreement. He was starting to like this Sardar. Although he was being polite, the hatred in his words was evident. Bhola could work with him.

"What made you call us, Sardar?" Chachu asked casually.

Sardar Sauraga smiled. "I've heard tell of Sardar Bhola's deeds. People fear him. Even soldiers. Your gang is small but it's gained a lot of notoriety."

"And I hate Ananda just as much as you," Bhola

said, searching Sauraga's eyes for a reaction.

And the reaction came. His eyes lit up, an indecent smile curving his lips, "Exactly. You see, we recently got word that Ananda is returning to Nishanata in a month's time."

"So?"

"But he's going to take a detour to visit the Jagadhama temple."

This time, Bhola's eyes lit up. Jagadhama Temple was located in the Western Ghats across the plains. The temple was notoriously tough to reach, the path up the mountain dangerously narrow, meaning Ananda's retinue would be stretched thin. "You mean to ambush him."

The stranger had been right.

"Why did you reach out to me, really?"

Sauraga thought about it. Then shrugged, not wanting to hide the truth, "I sought advice from a travelling priest. He said you would be of help."

Travelling priest...

"And it's not like I haven't heard of your deeds." Sauraga chuckled and slapped his thigh.

Bhola nodded. "You have a plan?"

"I have people near Jagadhama who owe me from my performing days. I can sneak our men close to the temple."

This was their chance to nab the bastard.

"No!" Chachu grabbed control of the conversation, "Shedding blood in a temple will bring us bad karma! You want to rot in hell?"

Bhola clenched his fist, but it was Sauraga's sweet response that silenced Chachu. "No offence Chachu, but hell is the best we can hope for after what we've done. Isn't that right, Sardar Bhola?"

Bhola sneered, "*After*? The way I see it, Ananda's already thrown us in hell."

Sauraga chuckled in agreement.

Chachu's shoulders slumped. He had no response. He excused himself and left.

Rana signalled for three men to follow Chachu, then grabbed a leg piece, "Talk to him, Sardar."

"What?"

"Talk to him," Rana repeated, slower this time, "You're alive because of him. You're surviving because of him. Don't neglect his advice." He bit into the meat, its juices flowing down his greying beard.

Bhola grimaced, "And who are you to tell me that, Rana?"

Rana started at him straight. He held Bhola's gaze as he chewed on the tender meat, every passing heartbeat enraging Bhola even more. How dare this lowly bodyguard talk to him like that? It was only after he swallowed that Rana responded. "I'm the man who taught you to fight, *boy*."

The word stabbed him. Bhola wanted to strike Rana, but it was Sauraga who took offence.

Sword drawn, he held the blade at Rana's throat. "Apologise to your Sardar. NOW."

"Fuck off," Rana said casually, biting into the meat and chewing as if there weren't a blade at his throat.

"Say the word," Sauraga said to Bhola.

Rana swallowed, eyes still staring at Bhola. No matter how enraged he was, he couldn't let Sauraga kill Rana. "You hurt my man, and I will kill you myself."

Sauraga jeered, lowering his sword.

Rana licked his fingers clean and placed the plate down. He got up and wiped his hands on his pyjama, "I must see your Chachu. Sardar," he bowed to Bhola, "Sardar," he bowed to Sauraga.

"I'll join you," Bhola said getting up. Ignoring Sauraga, Bhola walked in Chachu's direction.

He caught up to Rana, deciding to stay silent.

Their men followed in a line.

Once out of earshot, Bhola said loudly, "If you ever talk out of line, I won't think twice before lopping off your head."

"That's the problem, *Sardar*." Rana turned and faced him, "You don't even think once." The former Pehlwan towered over him, ignoring the threat.

Before Bhola could retort, Chachu's voice grabbed their attention, "Not here!"

They exchanged glances—Bhola's angry, Rana's expressionless—then followed Chachu.

Once they found a safe enough spot, Bhola took charge. "We are doing this. I command it!"

"It's too risky! And I'm not just speaking about bad karma!"

"You're acting like a coward!"

"And you're acting like a fucking child!"

Chachu argued all night, but Bhola's determination was unshaken. Bhola saw a chance at vengeance and he would get it no matter the cost.

"How long do you expect me to be a dacoit!?" Bhola yelled.

"Until we have enough to start over!" Chachu screamed back, "Even the great Gendaka Household was once a dacoit gang! They played their moves correctly and now they're nobles." Chachu grabbed Bhola's vest and pulled him closer. Bhola could see the pain and regret in Chachu's eyes. "I taught you to survive, boy. But this is suicide!"

Bhola shoved Chachu back so hard that Chachu fell on his butt. "You taught me to be a dacoit. You want us to change our ways now?"

"We can earn enough to stop this. Become nobles again! You can avenge your father then. Dethrone Ananda! Don't do this, Bhola." Chachu was on his knees, his hands joined to beg, "Please, Bhola."

"Dacoit, noble, how does it matter, Chachu?"

Bhola dusted his wrinkled vest, "Revenge is revenge." He pointed an accusing finger at his uncle, the snake tattoo looking like it was ready to devour him, "You promised me vengeance."

"Not like this…"

"SHUT UP!" Bhola shouted. "If you don't agree, you're free to leave."

Chachu went pale.

"LEAVE!" spittle flew from his mouth as he screamed, "Leave before I slit your fucking throat!"

Shaken to his soul, Chachu got up. He was about to make one last attempt but decided against it. Bhola saw a glint of tears in Chachu's eyes. It twisted his guts almost as much as the image of his dying father had.

He saw Rana run behind Chachu, but Chachu said something to him and gestured him back.

Rana came up to Bhola and said, "He's really leaving, boy."

"Want to join him?"

Rana's expression was rock-like as ever. "He ordered me to stay and protect you."

"Fine." Bhola said through clenched teeth, "Then plan the ambush."

Rana studied his eyes. After a moment, he nodded.

Jagadhama Temple was one of the eighteen ancient pilgrimage spots for devotees of Jagarakshaka. It was the least visited, owing to its location. Only devout priests and green youngsters desperate for blessings visited this place. The difficulty in accessing the temple even prompted some not to count it as a mandatory pilgrimage, further limiting the number of visitors.

All this meant that Bhola could place enough of his dacoits in the temple complex for the ambush.

The temple complex was situated on the top of the tallest peak in the Western Ghats. The mountain path that led to the temple twisted and curved like a mad snake, forcing large groups to pass in thin files.

The monsoon had painted the mountains lush and green. The air high above was cold and humid. Sauraga had arranged for threads that their men could use to disguise themselves.

A quaint village at the mountain's foot served as the last point of rest before the trek to Jagadhama. The dacoits had reached it almost a week before Ananda's estimated arrival to set up their ambush.

As per Rana's instructions, all twenty of Bhola's men had taken shelter in the temple, claiming to be refugees seeking Jagarakshaka's protection. The ever-generous priests who let them in didn't even think to search them. After all, who would be cruel enough to shed blood in a temple?

Sauraga's men, on the other hand, found precarious footing off the mountain paths. They had hauled up enough soil to create a small rockslide to cut off Ananda's already-scant numbers. Rana's plan seemed flawless.

As if to bless them, Jagarakshaka even ordered the rains to thrash the mountains on the day of the bastard's arrival.

Rainfall obscured their vision. Bhola and Rana hid in a tree, giving them a vantage point of the temple's entrance as well as the path leading up to it.

Storm clouds rumbled like war drums, making Bhola restless. "He won't call it off, will he?"

"The man's as devout as a priest," Rana said, "He'll walk barefoot over burning coals if it means pleasing the Gods."

"Have we received word of their departure?"

"He'll come, boy," Rana said, "Be patient."

The path was thin, the mountain on one side, a thorny fall on the other. Hidden deep within those thorny shrubs and mossy rocks were Sauraga and his men. They would climb out when Bhola gave the signal. They were so well hidden that even Bhola couldn't tell their exact positions.

Almost an hour later, when the rains tired out, Bhola spotted a small entourage in the distance. It was still half an hour's march away from the temple, but he could see Ananda's dampened flag.

His revenge was coming to him.

Ten minutes later, Bhola heard the rockslide. The rains had slowed to a drizzle, allowing them to hear the soldiers panicking. They rushed to clear the path, but their numbers weren't enough. A few moments later, Bhola saw a smaller retinue depart. They had a golden parasol among them.

"That's Ananda, isn't it?"

Rana shrugged, "Could be a decoy. Kings use decoys often." He turned to look at him, "You want your revenge, boy? Don't do anything hasty."

For the first time in years, Bhola nodded in submission. He would kiss Rana's feet, he would surrender himself to his Chachu and beg for forgiveness as long as he could kill Ananda and get away with it.

His heart thumped as the small retinue of twenty soldiers, ten attendants, six royal guards and two advisors came into view. The king wore bright white robes, as was expected of pilgrims who wished to perform a *puja*. It was easy to keep an eye on him.

"Twenty-eight armed men," Bhola said.

"What makes you think the servants aren't equipped to fight?" Rana whispered back.

Bhola felt something touch his leg. Startled, he looked over his shoulder to see a snake slither by. He sneered. *Jagarakshaka, protect me.*

"We're outnumbered," Rana said, "I'm signalling for backup." He proceeded to whistle a bird call.

It wouldn't be necessary. "Get ready," Bhola said, already prepared to jump down.

Ten soldiers entered the temple gates while the king waited for his servants to prepare his offerings. Immediately, a lone soldier ran out of the gates and conferred with the advisors.

Bhola could sense something was wrong, but his belief kept him calm. *Durajaya, destroy my enemies!*

The advisors approached the king, who looked offended. He shouted at them, seemed like he was reprimanding them. Then, he proceeded to walk straight. Bhola heard him say, "Trust the Protector!"

Ananda entered the temple complex, followed closely by his hurrying retinue. Bhola sneered and gave the call. High above, the sky rumbled again. The rains would pour and the clouds would weep as a bastard's blood was spilt on sacred temple grounds.

Bhola and Rana carefully slid down the tree. They slowly made their way towards the entrance, where four soldiers stood guard.

"Wait for backup," Rana said.

Bhola ignored him, grabbing the sword he'd hidden under the tree. He unsheathed it and darted towards the guards. He surprised one guard by slashing his throat, kicking the second between the legs while slashing at the third.

The fourth one raised the alarm.

Bhola managed to cut the fourth one down while the second and third took defensive stances. Rana drove through one. Bhola cut down the other.

Rana looked at him and simply growled.

"Backup."

Bhola saw Sauraga climb off the sides of the cliff. Far in the distance, battle horns erupted amongst the growing drizzle. The ambush had begun.

Bhola turned to see the soldiers rush to the entrance. Two against ten was going to be tough, but the disguised beggars inside the temple would even their odds.

All hell broke loose.

Ananda's men were disciplined, forming defensive positions around their king. The dacoits howled savage battle cries to aggravate the chaos. Swords met in heavy clinks. Men groaned. The air burgeoned with death.

The royal soldiers had better armour, better shields. The dacoits had only their blades and wits. Bhola saw his men fall one after the other as their disorganised attacks failed to shake the king's men.

Bhola gripped his sword tighter as he noticed Sauraga and his forty dacoits approach the gates. Swords drawn, Sauraga dashed forward.

"KILL THE KING!" Bhola screamed, his cry met with a howling chant from the dacoits and a flash from the storm clouds above.

Thunder echoed as the dacoits crossed the gates. The royal guards braced for contact.

Bhola deflected a blade and shouldered a soldier straight in the face. As he stumbled, he grabbed the man's vest and flung him to the side. He parried a third and arced the sword away. It had been some time since he had fought such disciplined men, it was almost exciting.

Bhola played with his opponents before swinging into a flurry of cuts so rapid that the soldiers couldn't keep up. Another joined to aid him but Rana ran through him with his sword. He pulled out the bloody weapon with ease and chopped straight at

Bhola's adversary. The cut took the soldier's lower leg; he fell to the ground, Rana's sword following soon after to stab straight in the chest.

"Don't play around boy!" Rana shouted, turning his attention to another soldier.

The disguised beggars had taken to slaughtering the innocents, making sure that chaos reigned in the temple. They continued to scream and howl as if they were possessed by demons, all according to Rana's instructions. Half of them had fallen, but the rest managed to hold their own.

The rains poured harder, obscuring their vision. The thrashing rains doused out the sounds of metal against metal, of injured and dying soldiers. Even the Gods couldn't bear witness to the outrage of this ambush.

Bhola pushed through Ananda's soldiers, not caring for the cuts that stripped his vest. He accepted every attack as if it were nothing, countering with fiercer, deadlier blows. Rana backed him up, keeping the guards away. Soon, the dacoits had outnumbered Ananda's men.

The last round of defenders around Ananda made a semi-circle, shields almost interlocking to create a barrier between the killers and their king.

"You dare spill blood in Jagarakshaka's abode?" Ananda shouted, his voice booming over the battering rains.

Bhola could barely see the man's face. "Fuck you! You took everything from me!"

Ananda threatened, "Drop your weapons now, or my son will kill you all!"

Bhola frowned. "Didn't you hear what I said? This is revenge for my father! For my family! For my city and its people!"

"What city? You really think I go around pillaging every place I conquer?"

"You gave the order!"

"If you had come to me, I could've given you justice!" He stepped forward and Bhola saw his face. An ageing man, clean-shaven. He had tired eyes but stood with his head held high. "Instead, you resort to such *blasphemy!*"

"Don't get distracted," Rana cut in, "Let's get it over with."

Ananda drew his sword and signalled the charge, "*Akraman!*"

From behind, the king's men returned the cry for attack. They had managed to cross the rockslide.

Bhola's hopes fell. *No. NO!*

Bhola dashed forward, spearing through two soldiers. He was a raging bull let loose. He almost made it. Ananda was just a few steps away.

It was now or never.

Sword ready to strike, Bhola gauged the king's defence, only to be knocked aside by a guard.

Bhola stumbled briefly, directing his rage to the guard who pushed him. He cut him clean from the midriff and turned to look at Ananda with blood-red eyes. Mouth foaming with anger, lungs burning, heart racing, Bhola wasn't himself.

All he felt was hate and fury. And he unleashed it.

Ananda stepped back as he parried the first two slashes. The third cut Ananda's leg. Bhola did not stop. His arm ached with the constant motion, but he did not care. One slash at the torso, one arc away from a riposte to cut on the bastard's side. Bhola did not stop.

Finally, Ananda managed to stab through Bhola's attack. Bhola simply grabbed the sword with his free hand and saw an opening. *NOW!*

A flash of lightning.

Bhola stabbed, straight into Ananda's heart. He saw the bastard's eyes bulge as his heart exploded.

Thunder rumbled.

Blood gushed out of his mouth, washed down by the rain. Bhola left his grip on Ananda's sword. It fell to the ground with a clang. Bhola drove his sword in deeper as his father's killer tried weakly to stop the sword.

Finally, Bhola pulled. The sword slid out, a spray of blood painting his face red. The stinging blood rain reminded him of his father, of how he'd begged. "Beg!" he spat.

Ananda stumbled and fell, trying weakly to stay up. Bhola saw his neck showing through the robes.

Bhola's mind flashed back to the image of his father being decapitated. He raised his sword, positioning himself to behead the king in a single arc. *NOW!*

Bhola suddenly felt light. He lost balance and fell to the bloody ground, his sword clanging before him. His severed hand slapped at his face.

The pain followed next. Fire burned through his right hand, his left instinctively trying to put pressure on the stump. Bhola felt his insides churn. His mind cried in anger and desperation. "NOOOO!"

He felt another stab in his back. He was so close to revenge... all was lost.

No! Bhola saw two guards rush to care for their king, but Ananda's white clothes were dyed red.

The king was dead. Bhola closed his eyes and accepted his faith.

"FATHER!"

No one cupped his mouth. Who was screaming? Who was crying?

Bhola opened his eyes, realising that the dacoits were losing. He saw Sauraga's headless body sitting against the temple gates. He searched for the voice that had screamed and saw a young man bent over the dead king.

"FATHER! NO!" he screamed. Prince Ina, Bhola realised. A son who lost his father. But no one cupped his mouth. He hadn't lost everything, just a father.

Just a fucking bastard of a king who happened to be his father.

"WHO DID THIS!?" Prince Ina demanded, his voice loud and ready to kill.

"That's the man. He's the Sardar of this gang," someone said.

Ina walked over, sword ready to kill. But he stopped. "Arrest him. I will make an example of him." He turned, "Gather all the surviving dacoits. No one can get away with this. NO ONE!"

The surviving dacoits were taken to the village, where Ina delivered his promise.

First, their limbs were chopped off, one by one, one joint at a time.

Bhola's mind broke by the time he lost his remaining hand. How could the Gods favour such cruel men? Why was he cursed to suffer like this?

To prolong their suffering, healers were stationed nearby to make sure none of the dacoits died of shock, bleeding, or any petty reason. There were only twelve survivors, meaning a lot of work for both torturers and healers.

After a week of torture in public, those limbless dacoits were tied to stakes and stoned until they lost consciousness. When they awoke, rats, crows and maggots feasted on their festering wounds.

As if by the Gods' curse, Bhola was the last remaining dacoit who refused to die. Pinned to a stake for public warning, he let his broken mind ride through happier memories. He refused to accept that he had ever become a dacoit. This was just a nightmare. He would be up soon.

Maa would greet him at breakfast with his sister. Baba would take them out for a hunt, maybe make a picnic out of it. They would have a happy day. A happy life.

"You did well, Bhola."

Mind struggling to react, Bhola opened his lone eye. Below on the ground, shrouded by darkness, stood the stranger. Pain and suffering were replaced by anger. "Why...?" his voice was weaker than the string by which his life still hung. "Why...?"

"You're an unfortunate nobody, Bhola. A pawn in a game that's been in the works for centuries," the stranger came close, hands glowing. "I just needed you to kill Anandananta. I didn't expect his son to be this..." the stranger shook his head.

"Who...?"

The stranger looked at him, then smiled. "I go by many names. But if you want to know who sent you to die... it's Jagarakshaka."

Bhola's weak heart began beating slightly faster.

"Everything I did, everything I set in motion, it's for the good of Adeva. You played your part well, Bhola. For that, I will grant you a swift death."

Bhola had barely digested that thought before the stranger pointed his open palm in Bhola's direction. The glow grew blindingly bright.

The last thing Bhola saw was white.

The next morning, the last dacoit was declared dead. The dacoits' rotting corpses were finally set ablaze unceremoniously.

Chachu looked at the twelve stakes, not knowing which of them had been his nephew. What had happened was horrific, but no one would ever blame Prince Ina for his reaction. He was just a grieving son who took revenge against the monstrous dacoits who dared to spill blood in a temple. They had gone so far as to kill the priests and innocent pilgrims too. Of course, such wicked deeds had to be castigated. The severest of punishments wouldn't be enough. Even in death, the vile dacoits would suffer as their souls were tormented in hell for eternity.

Chachu's heart broke that day. He lost his will to live, knowing he was responsible for his Bhola's death. He had failed his brother, his family, and his nephew. Now his family's name would be forgotten.

Chachu had barely eaten anything since learning of his nephew's fate. He had arrived just that morning. He didn't know if he could count himself lucky not to witness his nephew suffer. He tried to convince himself that Bhola had died in the battle, and they lied to the public about the real Sardar. But deep down, he knew it was unlikely.

And now, as the sun set behind him, he looked to the pile of ashes that was once his nephew, and his dacoit gang.

It would've been kinder for Bhola to have perished in that fire all those years ago.

Chachu said a silent prayer to the Gods. *Forgive me, Jagarakshaka. Please give my nephew some peace in the afterlife.*

This story was first published in Dark Horses Magazine Vol 22, Nov 2023

BITTERSWEET CHUTNEY

Puratshah Kingdom
A few years before King Sangaar's coronation

Prologue

"**C**ome here, Poorna," her mother's voice was as sweet as honey. Her presence was like hot soup on a cold winter evening. "Let me teach you how to make my grandmother's famous chutney."

Poorna ran to her mother with excitement. Her onion tamarind chutney was one of Poorna's favourites. She loved it so much, she used to drench almost everything in it. And now, she was going to learn the recipe!

Poorna memorized each ingredient, recognising the home-grown tamarind, mint and chillies. The onions, her mother had purchased after much bargaining from the bazaar. The rest, her father would buy and stock up every other month. She was familiar with the kitchen, not because she was expected to be, but because she liked it.

"You know, my grandmother once told me that the king himself was pleased when he tasted her chutney! He even offered to pay her a fortune for the recipe, but she refused. Family secrets aren't for sale." Poorna loved that story. The fact that her grandmother had rejected a king made it legendary.

Her mother took less than half an hour to make the chutney, and that fascinated her more than anything else. Something so delicious, yet so easy to make! No wonder the recipe was a secret. You wouldn't want everyone making this magical chutney in their homes.

Once it was ready, Mother offered Poorna the first spoon for tasting.

Bittersweet, perfectly balanced, like all things should be. So simple, yet the explosion of flavour could enrich any dish served.

Poorna was seven when she first made the chutney with her mother. Within a month, she learned how to make it by herself. By the time she was to be married, her mother claimed that Poorna's chutney had somehow begun to taste better than the family recipe.

When Anna had come to see her as a potential bride, it was Poorna's chutney that impressed his family. Of course, Poorna had a lot of qualities, but it was the aftertaste of that chutney that Anna would bring up again and again till the end of his days.

She was glad that he lived just a village away. That meant the ingredients in the kitchen wouldn't change much. Her food was so good that Anna often teased her that she should start an eatery of her own. With both of them earning a living, their family could live like rich folk.

Although the thought of running an eatery was

daunting, she did fantasize about it from time to time. She would imagine being in an eatery's kitchen as she continued to make all of her favourite dishes, including her mother's chutney.

That chutney would come to define Poorna's life. More than she could ever imagine.

I

*"Take half a bowl of tamarind pulp,
1-2 finely chopped onions,
3-4 green chillies, 1 bunch of mint leaves,
black salt and white salt."*

Poorna had two children, Chaitanya and Svarnali. She liked to call them by their pet names—Chikoo and Sonu—so much so that their real names sounded awkward on her tongue.

She hadn't believed it when people told her that her children would become her life, but now if anyone asked, she could do anything for them.

Poorna was busy serving breakfast to her children when her husband's voice interrupted their chat.

"Poorna! Poorna!"

Poorna almost jumped, "What is it?"

Anna ran into the kitchen, sweaty and breathless.

"Anna!" she scolded him, "Catch your breath before you speak." She stood up and fetched water in a clay cup.

Chikoo whispered something to Sonu, who started giggling. Poorna wanted to get in on the joke, but her husband didn't seem to care. "The king...!" he huffed.

"The king can wait!" she said, offering him the cup. Poorna made a face at Chikoo and Sonu, prompting more giggles.

Anna accepted the cup and drank half a sip before finally catching his breath. "The king has been blessed by the Gods!"

Poorna put her hands on her waist. "Aren't all kings blessed?"

"But Raja Shahapasa is here! In our village!"

Poorna raised her brow, "When did he get crowned?"

The entire village, man, woman, children, even the animals gathered at the village centre. The king's retinue had erected the Puratshah flag. However, it wasn't the white floral flag of the ancient mountain kingdom; this one was golden, the older, more ancient design. Poorna could never have recognised it if it weren't for Anna.

The crowned noble underneath that fluttering gold flag was a pale and skinny man. His attire wasn't half as regal as a king's should be, and his demeanour even less so. He stood with a hunch as if the weight of the ancient Puratshah Kingdom was too much to bear. His movements were jittery, his fingers twitched in a rhythm independent of his eyes' rapid blinking. Even though they stood at a distance, Poorna could tell this man was sick.

Suddenly, he stood straight up and punched a bolt of lightning into the air.

The village—seemingly the whole world—grew silent.

Poorna went pale, not sure what she just witnessed, but she didn't have time to think over it. The king had begun speaking. Sonu dug her face in Poorna's stomach, while Chikoo looked at the display with fascination.

The king's voice boomed like thunder as he spoke. But he spoke in the dialect of royals, and Poorna didn't understand it clearly. There was a royal translator there, but Poorna couldn't get herself to pay attention. What did it matter who sat on the throne? She didn't care which king she bowed to as long as she could live safely in her home and give a good life to Chikoo and Sonu.

Poorna almost jumped in shock as the crowd ruptured into cheers. The king had said something powerful, it seemed. She turned to her husband, who was screaming his guts out in support of the new ruler. Sonu clutched at her sari, while Chikoo joined his father in cheering.

Poorna finally managed to grab Anna's attention. "What is he saying?"

Anna clicked his tongue as if she were a kid asking a stupid question. "Are you deaf or what?"

Poorna frowned, but Anna didn't notice.

"The old king is dead," he said half distractedly. He wanted to continue listening to the speech. "The new king has been blessed by the Gods!"

So what? Why is everyone cheering? Just as Poorna turned to look at the king, he raised his hand and a burning white glow emanated from his fist.

"Blessed by the Gods!" Anna shouted, "Long Live Raja Shahapasa!" He wasn't the only one screaming. The entire village erupted in cheers.

King Shahapasa shot bolts of lightning into the air, heightening the crowd's high spirits. He continued to shout in his royal tongue, the translator relaying his words to the crazed crowd.

Poorna tugged at Anna's shirt, "What is he saying?"

Anna struggled to shout, "He will bring back the ancient glories! We will all prosper under the god-king!"

More cheers. Deafening.

Poorna smiled half-heartedly, not convinced. How could a man be a god? Yes, she had seen him shoot lightning bolts, but it could have been an illusion, like the magicians in fairs.

No, if Anna is cheering, it must be something worthwhile. After all, Poorna never listened to him when he spoke of village politics, the kingdom's news, or anything that didn't directly affect her, her children, or her household. She didn't know enough to be doubting this man. Maybe he was a god? Or blessed by them?

King Shahapasa shot another powerful bolt of blinding light into the sky. The clouds parted, birds flapped away in panic, and the people met that display of divine power with a chilling round of applause.

"Jai Shahapasa! Jai Shahapasa!" The chant echoed across the village. *Praise be to Shahapasa.*

It was frightening. Poorna knew that kings could influence people, but this was the first time she was seeing how deeply that held true. She saw her entire village—the potter and his wife, the Sarpanch and his family, the newlywed couple from across the river, the herdsmen, hunters, farmers, friends and foe, rivals and acquaintances, everyone united by their admiration of this one god-man. *God-king*, she corrected herself.

Her thoughts were interrupted by Sonu's crying. The poor child was probably terrified. Poorna picked her up and consoled her. Despite her own qualms, she smiled a fake smile, finally managing to quell Sonu's tears.

Not wanting to be left out, Poorna joined the cheers. "Jai Shahapasa!"

The god-king continued to speak, and Poorna continued to cheer without knowing what he said. But the crowd was pleased, and if he appealed to so many people he must've been saying something right.

After his speech, the god-king sat in his opulent chariot and his procession moved to the next village. Poorna's throat went dry as she screamed her half-hearted farewell along with everyone in her village.

By the time the energy died down, Poorna's ears were ringing. She felt drained, but her emotions were still alight.

"Tonight, we shall celebrate!" Anna announced on their walk back. "A feast! I will get fresh mutton from the butcher!"

Poorna, still recovering, smiled, "I'll make my mother's special mutton curry."

"And the chutney, right?" Anna asked hopefully.

Poorna smiled, "Of course!"

II
*"Grind the green chillies and mint
until they form a grainy paste."*

Months passed since King Shahapasa gave his speech. He never returned to speak with the villagers again. Poorna even doubted if he remembered the village's name. But Shahapasa's ministers came again, and again, and again. Every time, they sought the villagers' aid in making their kingdom great again. Grains, tools, volunteers, and sometimes even coins. The villagers happily complied. Even the poor provided a small portion of their alms in support of the god-king.

In those months, the kingdom announced a new branch of the military consisting of civilians. These civilians had the honour of being blessed by the god-king himself and would be eligible to live gloriously like warriors.

"The Puratshah kingdom had grown weak over

the years," Anna explained to Poorna, "But now Raja Shahapasa is growing our strengths. Isn't he so generous to let even the common folk join his army?"

Poorna nodded meekly, wondering why the kingdom needed another army in the first place. Whatever she could remember from her limited education, their kingdom had been pacifistic for the last two centuries. The other regions of Adeva had respected their decision partly because of the Puratshah Household's ancient lineage.

"Don't crinkle your forehead like that!" Anna teased, "Come now. Even if our kingdom were to go to war, who do you think will win? An army of mortals, or a god-king?" As if it were a joke, he laughed aloud. Chikoo and Sonu joined him, already daydreaming of a golden age, despite having no idea what it meant. They just didn't have Poorna's maturity to worry about reality.

"Are you planning to join them?"

"Jagarakshaka protect me!" Anna asked, "I can't do that! I have our farm and cattle to take care of. I can't just leave that all behind and join the Holy Warriors."

"Holy Warriors?"

"That's what the civilian wing is going to be called! You know, because Raja Shahapasa has blessed them himself!"

Soon, these Holy Warriors began patrolling the roads and nearby lands. Many of them would come to the village for food and other activities. They wore goldthread headbands over vermillion-smeared foreheads, something the villagers started imitating to show their devotion and love for the king. The coming of the Holy Warriors meant business started booming for locals offering shelter and food. It seemed like a golden age truly was dawning on the Puratshah Kingdom.

That was until rumours reached them that the king had allegedly usurped the throne.

"But Shahapasa is the elder brother," Anna argued over dinner, "the rightful heir! Anyway, his younger brother was studying to be a scholar. Why is he attempting to steal his brother's throne?"

"Why are we talking about this?" Poorna asked.

"You brought it up!" Anna said, breaking a piece of chapati.

"When?" The last thing she mentioned was how her mother-in-law had been kind enough to leave all her jewellery to Poorna. Anna had brought up how he was lucky to be an only child, which somehow he had connected to the king's sibling. Poorna remembered the whole conversation but chose not to add more fire to the argument.

"Forgive me for trying to talk about world affairs. The children have to learn, don't they? One day, I'll grow old, and they better be prepared to deal with the world!"

They were sitting on the floor of their tiny home. Anna's mother had passed away just two weeks ago. They had mourned her passing with bland food for thirteen days, which meant everyone was looking forward to this meal.

Roasted duck seasoned with pink salt and garlic powder, served with onions and her token onion tamarind chutney. Their first meal with spices and meat in thirteen days, and talk of politics had soured everyone's minds.

Poorna looked at her children, seeing worry draining their expressions.

"Can we please not talk about this?" She urged.

Her husband shook his head, "Why? Just because you come from a place that supports the traitor!"

Poorna's eyes bulged. "What are you saying, Anna?"

Anna chuckled, "Don't play the fool, Poorna. We all know his brother led the relief efforts in your village when the river flooded a few years back." He leaned closer to her, whispering, "Some men from your village were arrested by the Holy Warriors. Your village people are being called traitors."

Poorna's heart began racing. "Whose brother...?"

"Prince Shahawad!" Anna said, "Didn't he...?"

The name sent a shiver down her spine. Poorna knew who Shahawad was. She had even seen him help distribute rations. Poorna held her tongue, not wanting to start a fight by defending the kind prince. Tears welled up, but she wiped them away before they could fall. "I don't understand..."

Anna frowned, "I'm sorry. It's not your fault."

Poorna nodded, hoping the conversation had ended.

"Some people just don't understand. Stupid folks! Can't they see how much glory Shahapasa has brought us? He is a GOD!"

The energy in Anna's voice was alarming. He had shown interest in the kingdom's happenings before, but never with such passion. Ever since the new king had come to power, something within Anna had been awoken. Echoes of that sentiment seemed to plague their entire village.

"But..." she started, "he's a good man."

"Does a good man challenge the claim of a god?" Anna said, offended by Poorna's words, "Does a good man try to depose a god? No, Poorna!" he shook his head, "I hope none of your family is supporting that traitor! I wouldn't want the wrath of the Holy Warriors upon us."

"Why Baba?" Chikoo asked.

"Why?" Anna repeated, "Son, if you challenge a god, you are doomed. You'll rot in *Narak* for all eternity, with insects crawling on your face and snakes biting your legs, and—"

"Mummy!" Sonu screeched. Poorna seized the moment to reprimand her husband and end all talks of politics.

However, thoughts of Shahawad did not leave her that night. She dreamt of him, of an entire army led by him marching down on their little village and slaughtering everyone.

'Traitor!' her husband's voice rang in her head, *'you brought them here, didn't you?'*

'Why mummy!?' her children wailed.

Poorna woke up with a start, relieved that it was only a dream. But the terror did not leave her. She could sense a storm coming. She had to protect her children.

She had to make sure none of her family were involved in any traitorous activities.

Poorna spent the next few weeks trying to send letters back home. She couldn't read or write, so she had to rely on one of the village clerks to write the message for her. Since mail would only go out once a week, only the richer residents of the village could afford to avail of the service. Poorna had to spend half of her savings—money she had started saving to buy land for her eatery—to ensure her letter would be included.

She did not get any response for weeks. Every day that went by without a response, her fear worsened.

Had the letter been delivered? Were her relatives ignoring her?

The growing number of Holy Warriors in their village made things that much more concerning for her. She began hearing rumours of how the Holy Warriors exploited some traders, invoking their god's name when refused free services.

"The traders probably did something wrong. Why

deny a god anything?" Anna would say every time news of some atrocity reached them.

Poorna was too timid to admit her growing concerns. To her, even thinking that the Holy Warriors weren't as *holy* as they claimed was bordering blasphemy. She hoped that her husband's devotion would keep the bad away from her home.

She was wrong.

One day, when she returned from the bazaar, she found her house door open. Two soldiers with golden headbands stood guard. From within, she could hear her scant furniture and vessels being tossed around, interrupted only by sounds of screaming and threats.

Poorna went pale. Had her letter brought them here?

Chikoo and Sonu were with her, both of whom had frozen in fear. Between them, and her house, a crowd had gathered to observe the commotion. Poorna knelt and whispered to Chikoo, "Take Sonu and go to the river. Or the temple. Anywhere but here."

"But, Baba..."

"Just go!" Poorna said firmly.

Chikoo nodded and led his little sister away.

Once the children were out of sight, she stood up, ready to confess and save her husband. She took half a step forward when Anna walked out.

No, he didn't walk out. He was pushed out of the door, falling face-first into the veranda. Only when his assaulter stepped out with blood-soaked hands did Poorna notice Anna's condition.

The assaulter, a pot-bellied man with an unkempt stubble and intoxicated eyes grabbed Anna's hair and pulled him up to display to the crowd. "This man has betrayed the God-King Shahapasa!"

Everyone was silent. No one spoke a word or

moved a finger.

"He has conspired with the rebels. Now see what we do to traitors!"

Without warning, the two guards grabbed Anna's arms, outstretched them and chopped them off. These were clearly untrained youths because neither of their swings cut through. That only meant Anna's dismemberment would be excruciatingly painful.

Poorna watched with a tied tongue and wet eyes. What a coward she was. What a helpless, worthless woman whose stupidity had cost her husband his limbs!

Anna screamed as the guards finally ripped his arms from his torso—even after four swings, they still hung by a few tendons. They waved the arms in the air, displaying the extent of the punishment. Behind, Anna groaned and begged for forgiveness, "Jagarakshaka! Protect me, please! I'm innocent!"

Poorna immediately started calculating if she had enough money to save Anna's life. Could he continue to live on as a farmer? Maybe the village healer could reatt—

The pot-bellied Holy Warrior returned from the burning kitchen, holding Poorna's pestle stone. "Traitors deserve only one punishment!" He slammed the stone straight into Anna's head. Anna didn't even utter a syllable of protest.

The crack echoed in the air. The second crack slammed against Poorna's beating heart. By the fifth, Anna's head exploded, blood and brains leaking onto the veranda.

The Holy Warriors didn't stop there. They desecrated Anna's corpse beyond recognition. They burned the house and threatened to do the same with Anna's son. They declared they would hunt and rape his wife and daughter.

Fear clutched Poorna's beating heart. She wanted

to scream. She wanted to cry. She wanted this nightmare to end. But all she could do was keep watching as her husband's killers proclaimed hate and violence.

Jagarakshaka... what is happening to my life?

The house was now completely engulfed in flames, drowning out the Holy Warriors' threats. Finally, they left chanting, "Jai Shahapasa!"

Once they had disappeared, the crowd that had been so apathetic towards Anna turned with fear and sympathy to Poorna.

"Run away!"

"What god can condone this?"

"Bloody criminals posing as holy men!"

Poorna was too broken to let any of her neighbours' words reach her. She broke down sobbing, mourning her husband's death, cursing herself for even sending that letter. She was the reason Chikoo and Sonu would grow up orphans. Chikoo and Sonu would probably hate her.

"Think of your kids!"

Chikoo and Sonu...

"My children..."

Poorna found her children in the village temple. It was a small and cosy place that Poorna would visit at least once a week. Ironically, this was also the one place least frequented by the Holy Warriors.

The first thing Poorna did was embrace her crying children. "I am sorry, Chikoo, Sonu."

"Where is Baba?"

"BABA!"

Her children hadn't seen what happened, but they had certainly imagined the worst. Sadly, the worst had come true. But how was she to tell them?

How was she to confess that she was the real killer?

"I heard what happened," the priest said to her, "I am sorry for your loss, Poorna."

He offered her water while the junior priest offered food to the children. "Jagarakshaka is watching, children. He will protect you!"

Through stifled tears, Poorna asked, "What am I going to do now? I have no money. I have no home. I am sure they will burn our farm, and if they find us..."

"I suggest you leave the village," the priest told her, "I have a cousin in the neighbouring village, who might be able to help you temporarily. But I suggest you go to your native place. Or anywhere else. Just, not here."

Before she agreed, she took Sonu and Chikoo to see Jagarakshaka. It was a small idol, nothing fancy. But the temple had always been a place of peace.

"Forgive me, Jagarakshaka," Poorna said to the idol, "Please protect my Anna wherever he is. And please protect my children. I need your strength. I need your help. My life is crumbling, and we need you to intervene."

The idol did not respond.

III
*"Mix the paste, finely chopped onions
and salts with the tamarind pulp."*

Poorna left her village with a handful of coins and the clothes on her back. The temple priest, as promised, arranged for her and her children to hide in a transport cart heading to a neighbouring village.

In that village, the priest's cousin offered Poorna lodging in his temple quarters. In exchange, Poorna was tasked with cooking duties—the old cook had been abducted by the Holy Warriors and forced to cook for them. Narrating that story, the priest's cousin recommended that Poorna cook food that was subpar in quality to avoid a similar fate.

Poorna hated it, but at least she was safe. And her children were safe. She spent two weeks in that temple before procuring a ride to her native place. When she reached there, she found her parent's house abandoned. The neighbours said they went absconding just before the Holy Warriors had come searching for supporters of Prince Shahawad.

Luckily, the house was only vandalised, not burnt.

Poorna took residence in her maiden home, careful not to attract any attention. She pleaded with her neighbours to keep mum about her arrival.

Living in her maiden home wasn't as easy as she had thought. It was smaller than Anna's house, and thoughts of her parents' fate kept her awake at night. Why hadn't they informed anyone? Were they safe, or had they been abducted by the Holy Warriors?

What even was happening in the Puratshah Kingdom? These kinds of turmoil were unheard of except in news of other nations, and Poorna had rarely paid them any heed. All this growing tension was alien to her, aggravating her anxieties.

When she wasn't plagued by worries of the kingdom, she was drowning in guilt and sorrow over Anna's death. After all, she was the reason the Holy Warriors had attacked her house. They must've intercepted her letter and traced it back to her.

Those thoughts manifested into nightmares, where even her cousins, uncles, aunties, and parents had been caught and tortured like Anna. What if all her family had perished? What if she were all alone? How was she to keep Chikoo and Sonu safe?

Her worries found momentary peace when she

received a letter one day. She was grateful Chikoo could read it for her:

Sister. I know you're at Maasi's home. Two nights hence, I will knock to the rhythm of Durajaya's Third Canto. Be awake, and be ready. We will get you out.

As promised on the planned moonless night, when even the crickets did not chirp, there was a rhythmic knock on Poorna's door.

When she opened the creaky door, she saw a skinny man standing there wrapped in a black shawl, his face covered by a bandana and his head by a turban. It took her a moment to recognise Saikor's eyes. The sleeplessness in them made him look like a stranger.

She welcomed him in and gestured for him to sit in the kitchen, where she offered him dinner.

"Sonu and Chikoo..."

"I don't care," Saikor cut her, quickly regretting his disrespect. "I'm sorry, it's been a long day, and I must leave as soon as I can."

"The Holy Warriors don't patrol in the night," Poorna said, "I've checked a few times."

"I know," Saikor replied looking around the house, "But in these times it's best to be vigilant." He unwrapped the shawl, revealing his local attire. He looked much thinner than the chubby boy she had seen at her wedding. His face looked gaunt as he wiped the sweat with his bandana.

"I heard someone was staying at Maasi's house. I assumed it was you."

"Should I serve dinner? I saved you some food."

Saikor walked over to the other room where Chikoo and Sonu were asleep. Without permission, he walked in, checked that the sleeping figures were indeed his niece and nephew, and only then did he come and sit where she had arranged a *patda* for him to sit. "Sorry," he said, taking off his shawl and bandana, "It's best to be careful. I don't mind eating a little."

Smiling, Poorna began serving parathas, a healthy serving of spinach and beans, rice and daal. It wasn't enough and had gone cold, but she could see the hunger in his eyes. He hadn't eaten a full meal like this in days.

"You shouldn't have done all this."

"It's the least I can do."

He blinked rapidly, then nodded. She could almost feel his bliss as he mouthed the first morsel of paratha, filled with spinach and beans. He closed his eyes as he swallowed. After a moment, he asked, "Do you have that tamarind chutney Maasi always made?"

Poorna slowly shook her head. "I haven't made it this month. The kids don't eat like they used to."

Saikor nodded. "I heard what happened to you. I'm sorry."

Poorna clutched her sari. She chewed on her lip as he chewed on the cold parathas. Finally, she spoke, "Did you speak with the rebels?"

Saikor froze. He looked up and shook his head, "Don't even mention their names."

"But..."

"Poorna..." he sat up straighter, still chewing. The food wasn't fresh, but he still relished it. He finally swallowed the morsel and said, "You shouldn't have sent that letter."

Poorna felt a burn in her stomach. She wanted to explain herself, how she had just wanted to make sure her family was safe, that they had no connection with Prince Shahawad. But she couldn't. She clenched her jaw, and let tears wet in her eyes.

"Didn't your husband stop you?"

Poorna slowly shook her head, her husband's reprimands ringing in her ears.

Saikor sighed. "What's done is done. If not the letter, they would've found another reason to harm you."

"Is Amma…?"

"The Holy Warriors found them escaping." His voice was cold. "Your parents. Your brother. I was lucky I could help my parents out before they…" he stopped. "I'm sorry. I shouldn't blabber."

Suddenly, Poorna realised she was standing in a dead family's house. She started shivering. To live with uncertainty was excruciating, but learning the worst had happened was nothing less than soul-shattering. She felt queasy, her insides ready to spew out. She had killed her parents. Her brother. Everyone.

She couldn't believe how stupidly she had acted. How was she supposed to live with herself? She wanted to bury herself and die.

But she couldn't. She had to live on. For her kids. She had promised them a good life, and she would see it through, even if it meant she would have to live with the gross sins she had committed.

She cried until her eyes went dry. Then, she gathered herself and stood up. She had to be brave. She could mourn later when things settled down and the danger had lifted. She walked over to the kitchen's wash nook and splashed water on her face.

"Don't blame yourself, sister," Saikor said, getting up. "If there's anyone to blame, it's that mad god-king. Fuck him and his blind devotees!"

He walked over next to her. She stepped out of the way so he could wash his hands and mouth. "I'm telling you, you're lucky you weren't caught by those Holy Warriors. Bloody fuckers."

Poorna mustered up a question, "Why is he doing this?"

Saikor stopped washing his hands, "Doing what?"

"If he's a god then he should protect us. How can he let... how can he...?"

Saikor finished cleaning himself and wiped his hands dry on his vest. "Just don't talk about it. Not here. Not now."

Poorna bit her lip. She continued to stare at him.

Saikor walked over to her and whispered, "There are people in the king's court who're taking advantage of his madness. People think he's our saviour. The truth is, the divine power that he has gained... it's driven him mad. When a madman rules the world, madness becomes routine."

He walked back to his clothes and began tying his bandana.

"Brother..."

"It's time to leave."

Poorna's eyes bulged. "What?"

"We're leaving. Now. Get the kids up." He finished wrapping his shawl. "If I could find you here, so can the Holy Warriors."

Poorna grew stiff from fear. Her anger hadn't flared yet, but she asked, "Where will we go? What can I do?"

Saikor said, "You can join us. Join..." he lowered his voice, "Prince Shahawad" back to normal, "He will surely overthrow his mad brother and return peace to the Puratshah Kingdom."

Poorna's tongue had gone dry. She only wanted to leave the kingdom, but this was unexpected.

First, a god had come to their village. Their lives had turned upside down. Now she was supposed to dedicate what was left of her life to that madman's brother? if Shahawad were a good man, was it worth the risk of siding with the rebels?

"Think of your kids, Poorna. Your home is destroyed. Your village will be ruined by the year's end. If you really want to make a difference, help us. Help our cause."

"But what can I...?" Poorna's eyes fell on Saikor's plate. It was clean, not a speck of gravy or a grain of rice left behind. Of course. She could always cook for Prince Shahawad's army, just like she had cooked for that temple. She had managed to survive this long and always managed to find a way out.

Saikor wrapped himself in the shawl. "What will it be?"

She needed to clear one more thing. She asked, "I am responsible for so many deaths. Why help me?"

Saikor frowned. He rubbed his temple and sighed. "I'm sorry. I'm angry and sleep-deprived and very exhausted. But you are not at fault. You hear me? You are *not* at fault."

"But... I sent that letter..."

"I read a copy of that letter," Saikor said, "Only the most paranoid fucker would find something suspicious in there." He stepped forward and said to her in as kind a voice as he could muster in his urgency, "You acted out of fear, and they took advantage of you. Killing your husband was wrong. Killing your parents and brother was wrong. But if not your letter, they would've found some connection with me and assaulted them all anyway." He gently held her shoulder, "These people are demons, Poorna. They'll take advantage of the smallest of reasons to appease their animal instincts. So, stop blaming yourself, and start thinking of ways you can help!"

Poorna looked around the tiny house, her parents' home. Her temporary refuge of two months. She looked at Chikoo and Sonu sleeping soundly.

She had to do it. For a better life. For them.

"Let me wake up the kids."

IV

*"Add a few spoons of water
if the chutney is too thick."*

C hikoo and Sonu hadn't understood why their mother had woken them in the dead of night. Poorna was grateful they didn't question her, neither about where Saikor Mama was taking them nor about his dangerous-looking companions.

It took them a week to cross into Shahawad's territory, and there was noticeable relief in their group's demeanour once among allies. Another week passed and Poorna saw the huge base camp that Prince Shahawad had set up.

The camp sprawled across a few hillocks, resembling a small nomadic village. Almost every day, refugees would come here in search of shelter; Prince Shahawad did not refuse anyone. The madness that plagued the Puratshah Kingdom could only be defeated by compassion and careful planning.

Poorna prayed for Shahawad's success. Anna had been wrong. Shahawad was a good man.

"What can you do?" asked the man in charge of assigning duties to the refugees.

"I can cook."

He studied Poorna head to toe and she felt his gaze penetrate her soul. "Have you ever cooked for thousands?"

"No," she said, then firmly added, "but I can handle that."

"Soldiers, ready for war with an appetite to challenge an—"

"I can handle it," Poorna said, more firmly this time, "Whatever I can do to help."

The man continued to judge her. Finally, he nodded.

Weeks passed. Battles were fought. Many died.

Poorna continued to cook and serve, not knowing which of the youthful faces she was serving was having their last meal. It broke her heart to know that she was feeding soldiers who would, many of them, die for their cause. It broke her heart to be living among people who had all lost their homes and families to the madness of King Shahapasa.

Poorna had come to believe that Shahapasa was not a god. He was a demon, and the gods would punish his soul for the devastation he wreaked. She prayed for Prince Shahawad's success every morning and every night, first thing after her morning bath and last thing before sleeping.

She prayed to Jagarakshaka the Protector that he protect the noble Shahawad. She prayed to Durajaya the Destroyer that he give Shahawad the strength to defeat the mad god-king. She even prayed to Asma, the Creator who no one worshipped anymore.

She hoped her prayers would be answered soon.

A few more weeks passed. Chikoo and Sonu slowly recovered in Shahawad's camp. They started regaining some of their childly vigour. They made friends and started playing again. Sonu started cracking jokes and Chikoo got in trouble for his mischief.

Poorna welcomed their playfulness with open arms; her children were getting a better life now. There were even teachers who took care of refugee children. They worked hard to make sure all the children learned and grew so they could at least try and make something of themselves after the conflict ended. Poorna hoped this education would help her children do better than she could.

Poorna's skill in the kitchen earned her a promotion. While the Puratshah Kingdom was facing a horrible civil war, Poorna's life improved for the better. Of course, she couldn't really appreciate the growth because of the ungodly threat that forever loomed over them.

Even if Prince Shahawad was fighting for the people, his adversary was a god. What man, no matter how powerful, could stand up to a god?

Demon. Every time someone called Shahapasa a god—even when she herself referred to him as a god—she had to consciously correct herself.

Work in the kitchens was a good enough distraction from the pain and suffering of life outside. However, the ingredients they worked with had diminished over the past weeks. Even spices and essentials had become scarce. Whatever rich vegetables and meat they could get their hands on would only be cooked for the leaders and royalty.

Despite all that, Poorna's mother had taught her well. Every day, Poorna managed to cook a healthy delicious meal, no matter how simple or bland. The trick to a good meal was the right proportion of ingredients, even if it was a simple mix of salt and pepper. With her expertise, Poorna could gauge flavours merely by smelling the cooking pot.

The constant praise she received had rekindled her dream of starting an eatery. Maybe if Prince Shahawad dethroned the mad god-king, she could ask a favour. That thought made her work twice as hard.

Undoubtedly, her added efforts earned her a spot in Prince Shahawad's team of cooks. The closer she got to Prince Shahawad's person, the more news she received about how the war was progressing.

It did not look promising. Shahawad's resources

were being exhausted in protecting the refugees. He was losing the war because he couldn't afford it.

Everything changed the day he made a pact with the Rakshasas.

"They're humans!" Shahawad declared, "Tribals. They have their own ways. But they pray to the same Gods we do! Their blood is as red as ours. Tell me, my people! In trying times, would you rather submit to the madman who calls himself a god? Or would you embrace the kindness and hospitality of those different from you?"

The answer was unsurprising. The mad god-king had violently upturned everyone's lives. Even the aid of demons seemed rewarding.

And it was.

Poorna saw the return of spices and ingredients. The food they cooked was rich again, if only marginally. It was a small victory.

Slowly, the Rakshasas started sending their own food as presents, which further placated the doubters.

The notion that Rakshasas were seen as anything but humans felt stupid to Poorna. But not everyone shared the same sentiment. The doubters still retained their qualms, even if they stopped voicing them. She slowly realised that many of the refugees, despite being homeless themselves, continued to hate the Rakshasas as if they were in any position to discriminate.

However, everyone agreed that they had to make this pact if they were to survive.

Then one day, the war took a nastier turn. Suddenly battles erupted all over the Puratshah Kingdom. A new power had entered the game. That power, she later found out, was a mere sixteen-year-old prince from the Utpas plains.

A boy who was being called the Wild Beast. His

ferocity on the battlefield rivalled even the most savage of Rakshasas. His sharp mind and ability to unite people had gained him popularity, some said more than Prince Shahawad himself. What really made this boy stand out, however, was that he had faced the mad god-king in battle. He had been held captive for a month.

He had survived.

And now, he had allied with Prince Shahawad. They were in talks of finally ridding the world of the mad god-king.

Poorna was informed of a grand feast. A final celebration before they would execute whatever plan they had devised to depose the mad god-king.

Poorna believed this was it. She could feel the change in the air ever since this boy had joined the war. And she could almost taste the liberation that was sure to come. The Gods had answered her prayers and of all the thousands of refugees displaced by King Shahapasa's madness.

For the first time in almost two years, Poorna decided she would make her mother's chutney in honour of the boy's and Prince Shahawad's victory.

"You will not serve them," said the head cook, "You will greet the princes and make sure that they are being served properly.

"But..."

"We will all be there," the head cook assured her, "You don't have to be nervous."

Poorna agreed, knowing it could benefit her. Royalty was known to reward the poor if they found someone worthy of it. The added favour could help Chikoo and Sonu.

The feast was truly lavish, no expenses spared. Poorna got a sense that this was going to be Prince Shahawad's last attempt. It was all or nothing.

That night, she saw Prince Sangaar for the first time. Sixteen-years-old, he looked oddly older. As if the weight of a lifetime had sunk his shoulders. Yet, somehow, he maintained a smile on his face.

Poorna learned that day that Prince Sangaar had married a Rakshasin to bind their pact with the Rakshasas. So young, yet so thoughtful and mature. She wondered what kind of a person he was to have survived facing a mad god. *Demon!*

"Stop! Stop!" Prince Sangaar shouted, raising his voice. Poorna froze. His voice held a command that could match the madness she remembered from Shahapasa's speech.

"Is there a problem, my prince?" asked the head cook.

"What is this?" he pointed, and Poorna's heart sank. He was pointing at her chutney.

"My prince," the head cook smiled, "That's an onion tamarind chutney."

"Who made this?"

The head cook looked to Poorna nervously. Poorna braved her fears. "I did, my prince." She clenched her fist white, stopping herself from shivering or crying. "I apologise if it is not to your liking."

"Why are you apologising?" Prince Sangaar asked, "This chutney is divine! Please, get me more!"

Poorna's eyes bulged. "Of course!" she smiled with all her teeth. "Please, try it with the spicy mutton chops. And..."

"What is your name?"

Poorna blinked.

"Your name, sister."

"Poorna..."

"Sister Poorna," Sangaar got up, "When this war is over, and the mad king is de... deposed, I hope that the celebrations feature an abundance of this."

Poorna grinned like a little girl. "I will make sure there is enough for everyone."

V

*"Adjust the spice/sweet levels
depending on your liking and serve."*

The day the final battle took place, everyone in Prince Shahawad's camp prayed to the Gods. To Jagarakshaka the Protector, to Durajaya the Destroyer, some even joined Poorna to pray to the Creator, Asma.

Everyone prayed for Prince Shahawad and Prince Sangaar's victory over the mad god-king.

The skies rumbled. The screams of dying soldiers blended with the chaotic noises of battle, all echoing from afar. It sounded like the world was ready to end.

Poorna sat in her tent with Chikoo and Sonu, comforting them. The sounds of battle, despite being so far away, echoed ominously in the skies. The air in the camps was despondent. All hopes were pinned on this battle.

"Will Prince Shahawad win?" Chikoo asked, his voice meek.

"He has to," Poorna replied, "He has the favour of the Gods."

"What if he loses?" Sonu asked in a scared voice.

"Then Prince Sangaar will win. Why do you think two princes are fighting the battle?"

The two nodded their little heads, just as a loud rumble of thunder shook their tent. They could feel the tremors under them.

"Besides," Poorna quickly added to distract them, "Both Prince Shahawad and Prince Sangaar ate your mother's chutney. I prayed to the Gods so that my chutney could give them special powers!"

That seemed to sink in somehow, and the children grew less tense.

By the Gods' blessings, Poorna's prayers were answered. Prince Sangaar killed Shahapasa. A mortal man—a mere boy of sixteen—had slain a god. *Demon!*

For some reason, Prince Shahawad decided to surrender the throne to Prince Sangaar. Poorna didn't understand the politics behind that decision but trusted Prince Shahawad to have a good one.

As the mess of the battle was cleared, the refugees were brought into the city for rehabilitation. As part of Shahawad's team of cooks, Poorna and the kids were welcomed into the royal palace.

On the day of Sangaar's coronation, he gave everyone an audience, thanking each person individually for their aid, no matter how small.

"I remember you," he said, "The chutney woman!" He didn't remember her name, but he did recognise her, and Poorna didn't mind.

"Mummy's chutney gave you power!" Sonu shouted.

"Sonu!" Poorna reprimanded, but the king didn't seem to mind.

"Of course, it did! I ate three whole bowls that night!" King Sangaar said, rubbing his belly and smacking his lips.

Sonu giggled and Chikoo laughed.

Poorna smiled at the king.

"I'm sorry, I forgot your name. But I really do remember you," he said awkwardly, then continued, "I asked this to everyone who helped us, and I ask you the same. Is there anything that this lowly man..." he pointed to himself, "... can help you with?"

Poorna had been waiting for this moment. Ever since she had heard what the king was offering, she had known what she would ask for. "I want some money and a piece of land."

"Consider it done," Sangaar answered with a nod.

"I want to start my own trade."

Sangaar's smile diminished. "What of your husband?"

Poorna took in a deep breath and shook her head. *He's dead because of m... because of the mad demon-king.*

"Oh," Sangaar said softly. She expected him to mention that he had legalised widow remarriages, but instead, he said, "Whatever I can help you with, I will. Your name?"

"Poorna," she said with a smile. Immediately, she bowed with joined hands, "Thank you, my prince."

Sangaar knelt down to meet her kids' eyes. "Did you know, my mother was the one who raised me? While my father was off fighting wars, my mother made me the man I am today. A good man, and a good king. At least, I hope I am. Take care of your mother, kids. Don't trouble her too much." Sangaar rose to his feet and joined his hands to her, "Thank you for all your help, Poorna."

He moved on.

Poorna couldn't believe her fate. She had simply asked, and soon she would have her own trade. An eatery she could call her own. A trade that would help her raise her children and give them a good life.

It would be a tough task to maintain the trade, but she was ready to tackle it. She had come so far, she was bound to succeed.

Poorna hugged her kids and left the royal court holding a document with the royal seal that promised her exactly what she had asked for.

Epilogue

"**C**hikoo!" Poorna called softly, "Let me teach you how to make my family's famous chutney."

"Can I come too?" Sonu asked.

"Of course!"

A few years had passed since King Sangaar took the throne. A lot changed in the Puratshah Kingdom since. Some good, some bad. There were people who worshipped Sangaar like a god, while others criticised him for blaspheming and going against *dharma*.

Poorna didn't care for them. She had met King Sangaar only three times, but she was convinced he was a good man. A kind-hearted man who had killed a mad demon-king.

"Am I doing it right, mummy?" Chikoo asked. He was old enough to start helping with the trade. The local school had praised Sonu for her skills with numbers, which meant she could help Chikoo run the eatery better than Poorna had done since it started.

After all the hardships she had been through, Poorna felt like the Gods had rewarded her tenfold. That day when she first taught Chikoo and Sonu how to make the onion tamarind chutney was etched in her memory just as the day she learned the recipe herself.

That chutney had come to be the restaurant's speciality. King Sangaar even graced her with his presence the day she held a *puja* for its opening. He was her first customer even, and that had certainly played a role in its continued business.

Poorna couldn't believe how much her family's

chutney had come to define her life.

Not all lives leave a large impact on the world, and Poorna was one such. Even after being so close to one of Adeva's most important historical events, she didn't understand the depth of it. She wasn't an educated woman who could identify right from wrong. She was just a wife and a mother who wanted to live in peace, who till the end of her days would live with the guilt of her errors, and despite all would do her best to live a life that was peaceful because she owed her children that.

Poorna loved her children. She loved to cook just as much. To see her children actively take interest in her eatery was more than she could have asked for. She knew she had done something right. And after everything she had achieved, she knew that even if she were to die, her children would carry on with a good life.

Poorna had made a promise to give them a good life, and she knew she had succeeded.

THANK YOU, READERS!

I'm genuinely grateful that you read this collection.

If you enjoyed these stories, please consider leaving a review on Goodreads, Amazon, Storygraph or any other platform you use for book reviews. Reviews make a world of difference for indie authors like me.

Lastly, if you haven't already, you can sign up for my newsletter. I send just one a month, and it's a great way to get news about giveaways, deals, and upcoming projects.

You can sign up on my website:
www.ronitjauthor.com
Or follow me on social media: @ronitjauthor

Once again, thank you for reading!

ABOUT THE AUTHOR

Ronit J is a fantasy author and indie filmmaker from Mumbai. His debut novel, *Help! My Dog Is The Chosen One!* was published in December 2023.

He's a fantasy nerd with big dreams and bigger anxieties, all struggling to make themselves be heard within the existential maelstrom that is his mind. He also loves world cinema, chess, beer, food, and annoying his loving wife.

Ronit is currently working on a stand-alone fantasy novel titled *Island of the Dying Goddess*, before diving into his dream project that will begin on the continent of Adeva.

www.ingramcontent.com/pod-product-compliance
Lightning Source LLC
LaVergne TN
LVHW042158190726
843493LV00006B/1729